things
I wish I told
my mother

things
I wish I told
my mother

Susan Patterson
with SUSAN DiLALLO
and JAMES PATTERSON

CENTURY

1 3 5 7 9 10 8 6 4 2

Century
20 Vauxhall Bridge Road
London SW1V 2SA

Century is part of the Penguin Random House group of companies whose
addresses can be found at global.penguinrandomhouse.com.

Penguin
Random House
UK

First published in the UK by Century in 2023

www.penguin.co.uk

A CIP catalogue record for this book is available from the British Library.

ISBN 978–1–529–13686–9 (hardback)
ISBN 978–1–529–19907–9 (trade paperback)

Printed and bound in Great Britain by Clays Ltd, Elcograf S.p.A.

The authorised representative in the EEA is Penguin Random House Ireland,
Morrison Chambers, 32 Nassau Street, Dublin D02 YH68

www.greenpenguin.co.uk

My mom always said:
You're going to miss me when I'm gone!
Mom, I miss you every day.
—Sue Patterson

For my mother, Geraldine Katz DeResta,
who would have loved to tell her friends about this.
—Susan DiLallo

things
I wish I told
my mother

CHAPTER 1

RIGHT NOW, I AM standing thirty feet away from seventy million dollars.

Well, sort of.

Thirty feet from me, the key movers and shakers from Boujee Cosmetics are gathering in the mahogany-paneled conference room of my advertising agency, Vanessa. Several of them wave to me as they pass by— the president, the CEO, the director of marketing. This is not the first time they've been here.

And we're hoping it won't be the last.

Several months ago, the seventy-million-dollar Boujee account parted ways with its advertising agency. Suddenly ad agencies all over the city popped up like Whac-a-Moles, vying for the account. Most were eliminated in the first round (agency credentials and case histories) or the second (strategic development and media).

So now it's down to us and an agency in Dumbo, the cooler-than-cool section of Brooklyn. Today's the day we get to dazzle our clients-to-be with creative ideas on how to get all those Gen X, Y, and Zers to ditch their old shampoos, conditioners, volumizers, texturizers, lipsticks, moisturizers, foundations—and switch to Boujee instead.

That's where I come in.

You've probably seen all those rom-coms where a cute, pert, perky young woman (always petite and blond) lands the account by charming the CEO (always a man).

Well, that's not me.

At five foot ten, with shoulder-length brown hair and blue eyes, I can bench press half my weight. Well, half my *ideal* weight. Since my college swimming days—and my divorce—I'm at least ten pounds away from ideal. The curse of the ex-athlete a few years from turning forty.

Anyway, pert and perky is not how the game is played anymore.

These days, you have to learn a whole new Rosetta Stone–like language about "brand hash tags" and "brand conversation" and "authentic brand content."

I look at my watch. 8:25 a.m. Five minutes till liftoff. Sitting in my office, I mentally rehearse my presentation, from my opening remarks to what questions might come up and how I'm going to field them . . . when my phone rings.

At this hour of the day, it could only be one person.

I check the caller ID. I am right. It's Dr. Elizabeth Ormson, ob-gyn to the stars, whose patients include some of the wealthiest and most prominent women in the city.

Also known as: *my mother*.

Another daughter might let it go to voice mail, rather than be distracted. But that daughter does not know The Great Dr. Ormson. Ignore her call and minutes later she will call again and keep calling. My mother is a firm believer in doing things at her convenience, not yours.

So I pick up.

"I'm in the hospital," she says.

Four words into the call, and I am already annoyed.

"Mother, of course you are. You're a physician. You're *always*—"

"I checked myself into the ER late last night," she says. "I was just ending my shift when I started having chest pains."

"Wait. *What?* You mean, you've been in the emergency room since—"

"Yes," she says, cutting me off.

"Why didn't you call me *last night*?"

"Laur...*ennnne,*" she says slowly, using my given name—an indication that she is as impatient with me as I am with her. "I didn't *need* you last night. I need you *now*. I want to go home but they won't release me until someone comes to sign me out."

"I can't possibly do it now," I say. "I'm about to go into a . . . meeting."

I almost slip and say "an important meeting." But I know what her response would be: *Medicine* is important. *Advertising* is not.

"And there's no one else in all of New Jersey who can pick you up now?" I ask.

One by one, she knocks her friends down like bowling pins. One has shingles, one is in Miami, one is babysitting her granddaughter. I'm the last pin standing.

I grit my teeth. I don't want to go into this meeting angry. So I do what my therapist, Esther, always suggests: take a breath, then count to ten. Slowly.

"I'll be there as soon as I can, Mother," I say. "As soon as this meeting is over."

"Oh, fine," she says. "But hurry."

CHAPTER 2

"LAURIE MARGOLIS, YOU CRUSHED it! After you left, they said—"

"Hold on a sec, Drew. I'm in an Uber."

I tap on the glass partition. The driver is humming along to sitar music more suited to a yoga class than a drive to New Jersey.

"Could you turn that down a little?" I ask. He does.

"Okay, Drew. Now tell me everything." Drew Merrill is executive creative director of Vanessa. Fair, honest, a stubbled Brooklyn hipster with the required tattoos, and fiercely loyal to the people who work for him.

"They loved you. They loved your ideas. They had a couple of questions about timing and product placement. But they thought you had a really first-rate understanding of the hair-care category. Great opening line, by the way."

"Don't thank me. Thank Edith Wharton."

Good old Edith. Always there with a wise comment when you need one. As I stood up to speak, I looked around the table and quoted one of her mantras: *"Genius is of small use to a woman who does not know how to do her hair."*

They'd smiled. A few of them nodded.

And I knew right then that we were golden.

"They did everything but jump across the table and hug us," Drew said. "Turns out the Dumbo group didn't deliver. So—congratulations. The account is ours. Well, actually, *yours*. They insisted you be their key contact person."

Drew is a classy guy. He'd never discuss money or compensation on a cell phone. But I know I'll be getting a significant bonus for this. Maybe even a promotion from group head to creative director.

As my Uber pulls up to Ridgefield Hospital, I am still feeling good about myself. So good, even the thought of dealing with my mother doesn't bring me down.

(Esther would be so proud.)

The thick glass doors open automatically and I make my usual left toward the Walker Pavilion. Over the years, I have been here many times—as a patient (when I busted a finger playing touch football with a boy I had a crush on) and as a visitor. My father spent many weeks here, wasting away from pancreatic cancer, before we moved him to hospice care. So I know exactly which elevators will whisk me up to Room 723.

But when I get off the elevator and find my mother's room, I am in for a surprise.

No. Not a surprise. A shock.

I expect to see my mother sitting up, fully dressed in her usual designer clothing, tapping her fingers impatiently, angry about how long it's taken me to get here when there's no traffic in the middle of the day.

But no. My mother, the famous Dr. Elizabeth Ormson, is lying in a hospital bed in one of those white and blue hospital gowns, looking small and frail, and older than her sixty-eight years. Instead of frowning because I am late, I see a small smile begin to form on her face. And I am equally unnerved by her breathy, almost whispery words: *"You're here."*

My mother is connected to a bunch of machines. Red LED lights appear and disappear in sync, popping up and down. An IV bottle is dangling from a metal hook, dripping into a vein in her arm. Her blond hair, which she spends a fortune to re-frost every week, is splayed out on her pillow like a fan. Yesterday's makeup has caked on her face, and she has dark-blue mascara rings under her dark-blue Scandinavian eyes. A soft, insistent beep fills the room, as if counting out the moments of my mother's life.

This is not the mother I know.

Somewhere there's got to be a giant pod that contains the real, tough, feisty Dr. Liz Ormson. And in her place is this small, sad-looking woman with a pasty complexion and a bit of drool running down her chin.

But then she speaks. Yup—it's my mother after all.

"What took you so long?" she asks, sitting up. I am somewhat relieved. I think.

"And where are my clothes?"

I assume they're in the closet near the door. But I'm a little hesitant about getting them.

"Who told you that you were being released today?" I ask.

"Nobody told me. I'm releasing myself."

I should have known. I open the closet and hand her the bag of clothes the staff has "carelessly" (her word) crumpled up into a hospital plastic bag.

Yes, my mother's trying like crazy to get back to her usual take-no-prisoners self. But she can't quite pull it off. The hospital gown separates as she tries to remove it over her IV, and I get a quick view of her legs—thin, covered with varicose veins. For a split second, as she raises her hand to reach the call button, I see a small but unmistakable shakiness. But her trigger finger is working just fine.

She rings for the nurse. And rings. And rings.

"Mother, I can help," I say.

"No, Laurie, you can't. They need to unhook me. I'd do it myself, but the IV is in my dominant arm."

A short while later, a sweet chubby nurse named Remi enters.

"Well, my, my," she says, clearly surprised to see my mother tangled up, halfway out of her hospital gown and halfway into her beige Cardin sweater. "Where are we going in such a hurry, my dear?"

"*We* are not going anywhere. *I'm* going home," my mother says, like a finicky guest checking out of a luxury hotel because the room-service hamburger was too rare. "And I'll thank you to get me off this IV."

There is a touch—okay, more than a touch—of anger and hostility in my mother's voice. Nurse Remi doesn't seem to notice. She's still smiling. But her smile disappears as she checks the chart at the foot of my mother's bed.

"Has Dr. Akers said you could leave?"

"If I know Malcolm Akers," my mother says, "he's probably teeing off at the fourth hole at Somerset Hills. Now please disconnect me."

"I'm sorry, Dr. Ormson. You know the policy. I'm not authorized to do that."

"Then I'd like to speak to someone who is."

It's clear to Remi that my mother is used to having her own way about things.

"Yes, ma'am," Remi says, and disappears as quietly as she arrived.

Soon, the nursing supervisor—bigger, heavier, not quite as friendly, with several thick dreadlocks wrapped around her head—enters.

"What seems to be the problem, Doctor?" she asks.

"The problem is, I'm ready to leave."

Once again, my mother is told the rules. Once again, she rebels.

"Enough. We both know full well I can discharge *myself*," she says. "This is a hospital, not a prison. By law I am free to go as I wish. So now please unhook me from this IV, or I shall be forced to pull it out."

It is clear from the way the dials on the machine are jumping that my mother is aggravating her own body as much as she is aggravating us. But just as she's about to lose it entirely and start screaming, a wonderful thing happens.

The door opens. And in walks her cardiologist.

CHAPTER 3

DR. MALCOLM AKERS IS in his midforties, tall and stately as a tree, with dark curly hair. Like most cardiologists, he looks like he's in great physical shape.

"Hello," he says to me, extending his hand. "I'm Malcolm Akers." It's clear he overheard some of the conversation as he was walking toward the room. "It seems I may have walked in on a little ... kerfuffle."

I smile. I love that word. If only that was all my mother was: a chronic kerfuffler.

"Malcolm, this nurse," my mother says, pointing to Remi, "is refusing to unhook me. I need to be released this afternoon. I have my own patients to attend to, you know."

But Dr. Akers isn't listening. He's wheeled a PC into the room and is looking at her records. And then he frowns. "Not a good idea," he says, quietly. "Elizabeth,

I'm going to level with you. There were some irregularities on the EKG we did this morning."

My mother looks up. Surprised, annoyed, and—wait a minute. Do I detect a hint of fear? From the great Dr. Elizabeth Ormson? No. Can't be. I must have imagined it.

"Irregularities? Such as?"

He swings the PC around so she can read the screen.

"It appears you may have had a myocardial infarction at some point."

"Impossible. When?"

"Can't say for sure."

"I order these EKGs for my patients all the time, you know," she says. "And I know the statistics for false positives."

I have to smile. Who else but my mother would try to argue her way out of a heart attack?

"I'm sure you do. But you *did* present here last night with angina."

"Yes, but…"

"Listen, Elizabeth, you know as well as I do that—"

"Don't tell me what I know and what I don't!" my mother says. Wow. This is like watching a tennis match pitting Nadal against Federer. I take a step back to get a better view.

"Fine," he says. Defeated? Hardly. He bounces back like a Joe Palooka boxing doll. "We can't keep you here against your will. I know that. But the numbers show…"

And with that, they go into a quick medical shorthand discussion. I hear words like *arrhythmia…hypertrophy…ventricular tachycardia.*

"So I recommend that you allow us to do a few more tests before we release you."

She says nothing.

"*Strongly* recommend," he adds for emphasis.

I have to confess: there's something refreshing about seeing The Great Elizabeth Ormson taken down a few pegs. But then the tone of the room begins to change. As he goes on and on about Baseline Numbers, Just To Be Sure, Rule Things Out, he seems to be getting through to her. Slowly, she sinks back into her pillow, her spirits as crushed as the highlights on her blond hair. She looks the way she did when I first walked into the room.

And it breaks my heart.

"Tell ya what," I say after the doctor and nurse leave the room. "Stay here a bit, do what they tell you, and as soon as you get the all-clear and you're released we'll do something fun."

"Like what?" she asks.

"Maybe…oh, I don't know. Maybe go somewhere? Just the two of us. Would you like that? To take a trip with your one and only daughter?"

Too late. The words were out. And I see a sparkle in her eyes.

Oh. My. God.

What was I thinking?

CHAPTER 4

MY MOTHER LOVES TO travel. And she's done a lot of it. At a time when there were very few female gynecologists, she was in great demand and had speaking invitations from all over the world.

Come help us set up a prenatal clinic in Soviet Georgia.

Come talk to the women of Senegal about the trauma of genital mutilation.

Come to Lima/Cambodia/Colombia/Xinjiang and tell us about STDs/birth control/menopause.

Whenever my late father, a manager at an insurance agency, was able to take off work, he would join her. If her trips fell over school holidays, sometimes I would, too.

My mother was a great speaker. Calm, with a terrific grasp of her subject matter.

Not the warmest, perhaps, but certainly one of the most qualified. And besides, they weren't inviting her for her charm.

But the only time she and I traveled alone together was a total disaster. And it was to the one place you'd never think would fail: Disney World.

A kid's paradise, right? Well, maybe for other kids. But I guess Dr. Liz Ormson was just not a Disney World kind of gal. From the moment we went through the entrance gate, she seemed determined to tamp down the fun.

Rule Number One: No Going On Scary Rides. Any ride that went up and down, or round and round, or even the mildest loop de loop—anything more spirited than a carousel—was out of the question. I had just turned a very grown-up seven. Way too old for the kiddie park rides, I thought. So out of spite, I refused to go on anything.

As hundreds of kids walked by, munching on giant barbequed turkey legs the size of their heads, my mother shared Rule Number Two: No Turkey Legs. ("Who knows how long they've been sitting out in the sun, collecting bacteria?")

Perhaps the most crushing disappointment of all: I was not allowed to go on Cinderella's Golden Carousel. Too sexist, my mother said. "A smart, capable young woman waiting around for a rich man to come find her? I don't think so."

As I got older, nothing changed. Even a simple trip to the supermarket together could turn us into Mrs. Hatfield and Miss McCoy. Wegmans parking lot is where

I've learned, on various occasions, that I park too far from the entrance...spend too much on olives...buy the wrong brand of toilet paper...and should never put my purse in the cart.

"You know," I said to my mother once, "I'm really lucky. Some of my friends have mothers who've retired to Flagstaff or Boca. They have to wait months to find out what they're doing wrong. But with you around, I get to learn several times a week."

Yet here I am, planning a full fourteen-day trip away with my mother. And it's too late to turn back. I suggest a few places where we might go.

"I've heard good things about Iceland," I say.

"Too cold."

"Key West?"

"Are you serious? *Now?* In the middle of hurricane season?"

I cite various people I know who've just come back from India, Vietnam, the Galápagos, Manitoba, Newfoundland. My mother's reaction to all of these: "Why would anybody want to go *there*?"

Then she has an idea of her own. *Paris!* She seems surprised when I hesitate.

"I thought you loved Paris," she says.

I do. That's why I chose the most romantic city in the world for my honeymoon with Andrew—the man I divorced less than two years later.

"I have a better idea," I say. "How about Norway?"

Bingo!

My mother was born in Norway. She left for America when she was a teenager, and always said she wanted to go back.

I can see this excites her. I can hear it, too. Her usual wisp of a Norwegian accent becomes more noticeable when she says, "We could start in Oslo and wend our way up north by rail, to the glaciers."

Sounds good to me. I've always wanted to see the northern lights. "And maybe we'll even swing by your old hometown."

"I don't know about that, Laurie," she says. "But yes, let's go to Norway."

"Great," I say. "I'll start looking into fights when I get home. I mean, *flights*."

"And Paris first," she adds.

Say, what?

How did Paris get back into the mix? Maybe my subconscious was right: I *did* mean "fights."

But as she closes her eyes and begins to fall asleep, a rare smile on her face, I decide I can't bear to burst her bubble. This is a trip for *her*, not me. And she looks so happy.

So—fine. I'll go to Paris again. It'll be okay. I travel light. I will pack only what I need.

And I'll leave all my memories behind.

CHAPTER 5

THE SECURITY LINE AT Newark Airport is swarming with people who are determined to be comfortable when they fly. It's a rainbow of baggy sweatpants, leggings, and jeans, topped with sweatshirts from all the glorious tourist spots they've visited. I see a bunch of GRACELANDs, a couple of CARLSBAD CAVERNSes, one IN-N-OUT BURGER, and an entire family dressed in hoodies from the Lobster Pound in Ogunquit, Maine. Tons of boring place names. And one that makes me laugh out loud: the heavyset man wearing a shirt that reads, EXERCISE? I THOUGHT YOU SAID EXTRA FRIES.

As for my own outfit, I'm wearing dark slacks and an oversized olive-green sweater. Casual and sensible.

Once I'm finally through security, I gather my stuff and head to the gate. And there she is: my mother.

She's sitting on a bench with her legs crossed primly

at her ankles, wearing a Chanel suit that probably cost more than our combined airfare.

I have to admit, she looks great.

Under the fluorescent lights of the airport, her hair gleams with new blond highlights. She has gotten a manicure for the trip and, I would guess, a matching pedicure—although since it's October, the only person who will ever see her toes is me. She smiles when she catches my eye. Then she frowns when she sees what I'm carrying: my beloved beige duffel bag, stained with all the dirt, grime, and experiences of many wonderful trips abroad.

I doubt my mother sees it that way.

"You know," she says in her best Queen Elizabeth II voice, "at thirty-six, it might behoove you to invest in a real suitcase."

Behoove? That's a pretty fancy word for the way I like to travel.

I stand my duffel bag on its side, as if holding it vertically will somehow make it more attractive.

I see my mother is clutching a single black leather Louis Vuitton carry-on and a train case with silver clasps. A very elegant, very expensive two-piece matched set.

"Is that all you're bringing?" I ask her, surprised.

"Don't be silly. I already checked my big bags."

Correction: make that a four-piece Louis Vuitton matched set.

"And in case I buy too much to fit on the way home, I have a spare bag rolled up in here as well."

Of course she does.

This is not the first time we've experienced a bit of friction about this trip. The truth is, it's been a rough three weeks.

I should have known that any woman who has strong opinions about parking spaces, olive oil, and toilet paper will also have strong ideas about where to stay. While I scoured the internet for possibilities, my mother insisted on getting her travel agent involved. Janine of Elegant Journeys rose to the occasion.

"Janine says the Ritz has just undergone a $420 million renovation," my mother had reported. "She also has good things to say about the Mandarin Oriental, which includes a butler for every room, and the fabulous Georges Cinq, with its lobby desk staffed with sixteen concierges."

Did I mention that most of Janine's clients are on the top of the food chain?

Of course, like Janine, my mother also has strong ideas about where the hotel should be located: The classier, more upscale Right Bank of Paris, rather than on the definitely hipper, definitely woke-ier Left.

I shrugged my shoulders. It isn't the money. My mother can afford any of those. And when I travel on business and need the incomparable efficiency of a crack staff, guaranteed wake-up calls, and a concierge who can direct me to a restaurant loaded with Michelin stars, I'm a big fan of hotels. But to really experience a city, I much prefer a friendly bed-and-breakfast or an Airbnb.

Two totally different people. (Well, three, if you count Janine.) Two totally different philosophies.

But I may have found a brilliant compromise: La Figue Ridée, a three-star boutique hotel on the Île de la Cité, that charming strip of land *between* the Left and Right Banks, just steps from Notre Dame.

"The Wrinkled Fig?" my mother asked, translating. I have to admit: the name sounded better in French. But what won her over was that they offered to upgrade us to a suite. My mother agreed to give up one hotel star in exchange for total privacy.

By the time we board our SAS jet, we have put most of our disagreements behind us. I activate my out-of-office email reply, turn off my phone, and let out a happy sigh. Vacation at last. As I sink into my cushy business-class seat, I pride myself on being smart enough to seat my mother several rows ahead of me. My seatmate is a lovely French woman named Violette from Neuilly-sur-Seine, a fancy suburb of Paris. We chat briefly, and toast each other with a glass of complimentary Veuve Clicquot. Then we take off.

I am just about to pull out my noise-canceling head-phones, a blackout sleep mask, and my Kindle when the plane begins to shake a little. Then it shakes a lot.

A couple of wild vibrations later, the pilot gets on his mic.

"Sorry for the turbulence, folks," he says. "Ground control tells us we're heading into a bit of a thunderstorm. I'd like all of you to remain in your seats and make sure your seat belts are fastened."

I hear a bunch of clicks around me. Everyone is buckled in now, except one person a few rows forward, who starts to stand up.

I should have known—it's my mother, defying pilot's orders the same way she defies doctor's orders. *Now what?* Is she coming to check my seat belt? To remind me that drinking on a plane can be dehydrating?

But no. Grabbing on to my seat back, she leans over carefully and speaks to Violette.

"Would you be kind enough to switch seats with me, so I can be near my daughter?"

Violette, obviously touched by this motherly gesture, agrees. Once my mother is seated, she opens her purse and pulls out a very worn, very yellow scrap of paper filled with words in a shaky handwriting.

"I meant to show you this at the airport," she says. I begin to read it:

Bønn for den reisende: Gud, vær med oss i dag—våk over oss, forsikre oss mot fare. Beskytt oss mot skade. Vær alltid ved vår side av lyset, for å vokte, å herske og veilede oss trygt til vår reise. Amen.

"It's a Norwegian prayer for travelers," she says, turning it over to reveal English:

God be with us this day...watch over us, insure us against danger; protect us from harm. Be ever at our side to light, to guard, to rule and guide us to safety to our journey's end.

"Where did you get this?" I ask.

"My grandmother gave it to me," she says. "I've kept it in my wallet ever since."

She has? But here's the real surprise: she leans over to hold my hand.

She must see the startled look on my face. She smiles.

"You were always afraid of thunder, Laurie," she says. "Ever since you were a little girl."

She remembered!

I'm almost sorry I took an Ambien before I boarded. I would have liked to make this moment last a little longer.

CHAPTER 6

WHEN DID MY MOTHER learn to speak fluent French?

At Charles de Gaulle Airport, our driver meets us at baggage claim, holding up a card with our names on it. He is a total chatterbox. Before we pull out of the parking lot, we learn his name is Jean-Claude; he's married with a young daughter and has a son on the way. *("Un garçon! Un fils! Bravo le sonogramme!")* His wife, Aimée, had a C-section last time. And he is elated that Dr. Ormson, *la gynécologue célèbre,* assures him that yes, his wife will still be capable of a vaginal birth this time around.

As for me and my high school French, I can understand a word or two but it's too early in the morning to try to translate the rest. I would rather just look out the window and drink in the city.

I will never, never, never, ever grow tired of Paris. I've loved it from the first time I came here, the summer of my junior year of college. I love the clichés: the Eiffel Tower, berets, Pernod, even the nastiness of the shopkeepers who respond in English to my fractured French.

Even more, I love all the secret non-cliché places I've discovered: the bookstore where I bought *The Velveteen Rabbit* in French (*Lapin de Velours*)...the restaurant where I first tasted escargots...the little boutique in Montmartre where I spent a small fortune on the most amazing navy blazer with a red and gold crest—even when my friends back home told me I looked like a postal worker.

The City of Lights, known for its dazzling romantic evenings, is just as glorious at this early hour of the day. Storefront gates begin to slide open as we drive past. Even the elderly *fleuriste* in a ratty blue sweater sweeping the front of his flower shop looks like a character in a Truffaut movie. All of Paris is in motion, alive, calling out to me.

We finally pull up to the hotel.

I am relieved to see it's even more beautiful than its pictures...and even more relieved to see my mother smiling. (Point: Laurie.) A gorgeous glass door with brass handles opens into a white marble lobby with inlaid gold squares every five feet. There's a huge Belle Époque crystal chandelier the size of my first New York apartment. I am one dazzled tourist.

Jean-Claude kisses my mother goodbye on both

cheeks. Two doormen in red uniforms help us with our luggage. Neither of them shows any disdain for my lonely, dirty duffel bag. The Art Deco check-in desk is highly polished mahogany with a glorious patina. It smells of orange oil. A desk clerk in a crisp red jacket with a white carnation slides my mother's credit card through his machine. He hands us two five-inch brass keys that I could swear came from some nineteenth-century castle deep in the Rhône Valley.

Then we're whisked up to the eleventh floor. *To our suite!* Our bedrooms and sitting room are all paneled in delicate robin's-egg-blue silk, with matching drapes and magnificent eighteenth-century molding on the ceiling. A lacy plaster ceiling medallion crowns the chandelier.

It is so beautiful, even my mother seems pleased.

"Well, what do you think? Pretty nice, right?" I ask, hoping for some sort of compliment. *Silly me.*

"Get used to it. You're in Paris."

Our bedrooms are just off the sitting room. It is obviously preordained that I'll be sleeping in the smaller room. I could not care less.

I am all for getting under the percale sheets and the luxurious cashmere throw on my queen-size bed and taking a nap. But it seems the tireless Dr. Ormson has other plans. I hear rustling sounds coming from her room. A gift she's wrapping for me?

Hardly.

I pop my head in and see that she is slowly and painstakingly unpacking her suitcases, putting all her sweaters and lingerie into the top drawer of a wonderful Louis XV dresser. That rustling I heard was the tissue paper she puts between every article of clothing.

"Aren't you going to unpack?" she asks.

I stand and watch her, suddenly lost in thought.

"What are you thinking about?" my mother asks. I don't answer.

The last time I checked into a hotel in Paris I was with my new husband, Andrew, the day after our wedding. We stayed in a small, charming, family-run hotel on the Left Bank. When the owners found out we were newly-weds, they gave us the best room in the place: with a four-poster antique bed, a working fireplace, and a towel-warmer in the forest-green marble bathroom, and they put chocolates on our pillows every night. How we laughed when Andrew tried gallantly to carry me over the threshold. He barely made it before dropping me on the bed. With nothing but time on our hands, we didn't unpack for hours. Well, okay. Maybe days.

"So," my mother is saying, "if you're not going to unpack, we might as well take a walk around. Check out the neighborhood."

"Good idea," I say. And before she says what I'm sure she's about to, I beat her to the punch.

"But first, let me change into something nicer."

CHAPTER 7

I HAVE ONE COMPLAINT about Paris: If I lived here, I would probably weigh four hundred pounds.

Walking down the Quai de la Corse is a little like being a game piece on a giant Candy Land board. The street is dotted—should I say sprinkled?—with patisseries, each with the most gorgeous, glorious mountains of pastries piled four feet high in the window. And when you're tired of pastry, there are the chocolatiers. The smell of chocolate is everywhere. Who can resist all this?

Well, I know at least one person.

As I peek in the windows, my mother walks ahead, not at all tempted. I rush to catch up and make a mental note to stop by here again . . . alone.

She sits down at a small outdoor café and gestures for the waiter. Coffee seems like a good idea. But I'm in a dazed, jet-lagged mood, not sure if I feel like breakfast, lunch, or dinner. Fortunately, when you travel with my mother, she makes those decisions for you.

"*Deux cafés au lait,*" she tells the waiter, an elderly man in typical French waiter garb: black pants, a vest with pockets to hold change, a bow tie, and a long white apron.

"*Et une croissant avec un couteau,*" she adds.

I'm hoping *un couteau* is one of those pastries we just passed. Maybe something with custard? A napoleon? Some sort of fruit tart?

But no. The waiter appears with our order. Two coffees, one croissant, and *un couteau*—a knife that will be used to cut our one flaky, crunchy croissant in half.

The coffee, served in round china bowls with a frothy topping of cream, is rich and delicious. The croissant is buttery and warm. I finish my half in three bites as my mother is still on Bite Number One. She chews slowly as she looks around.

A group of young schoolgirls passes by, giggling. They are wearing uniforms—navy plaid skirts, white blouses, and assorted sweaters slung over their shoulders. One is classically beautiful—slim, Grecian features. One has long black braids, her face dotted with freckles. The third is plain with a too-large nose. But even that one looks classy, classic, put-together. My mother looks on, approvingly.

"It's amazing how even the youngest women here have such a sense of style," she says.

A perfectly appropriate comment, from anyone else. But coming from my mother, it's laden with hidden meaning that I have learned to interpret over the years. *"They look stylish"* is code for *"...and you don't."* A casual comment about another woman's hairstyle really means *"Don't you think you should consider getting rid of your bangs?"* That's the way it's always been with my mother. She says one thing; I hear something else.

I may not speak fluent French...but I do speak fluent *Ormson*.

"Something wrong, Laurie?" my mother asks.

"No, Mother. Why?"

"You look...I don't know. Sad?"

"No. Just tired."

"How can that be? On the plane I saw you sleeping."

She says it with a touch of disapproval in her voice. It's as if she is saying, "I saw you shoplifting."

"Yes, I slept. But not enough."

"Well, the first day of international travel is always the hardest," says my mother—for whom no day has ever really been too hard. I won't say she's led a carefree life. But her parents had enough money to send her to one of Norway's top private schools, then a first-rate college and medical school abroad. And her marriage to Martin Margolis, my kind, funny father who adored her from Day One, was the envy of all her friends.

My mother pays the waiter and drops a few coins

onto the plate. He bows and thanks her. Now I'm *really* ready for that nap. But my mother has other plans.

"Since we're so close, I want to walk over to Notre Dame and see what it looks like after the fire," she says.

I was afraid she'd say that.

"Do we have to?" I ask.

My mother looks surprised.

"I've seen pictures," I say. But that's not the truth. On our honeymoon, Andrew and I had wandered through Notre Dame, hand in hand. Both of us were moved by the solemn beauty of the place, the stained glass, the statues, the grandeur.

"Here's what we should do," he said as we were leaving. "Why don't we plan to come back here on our twenty-fifth anniversary, and renew our vows?"

"You won't have forgotten them by then?" I asked.

"Never," he said, and kissed me, right there on the Notre Dame steps.

I haven't checked the *Guinness Book of World Records* lately, but I'm pretty sure that was the world's shortest "never."

Eighteen months and one emotional affair (his) later, we were set to battle it out with attorneys until we realized a divorce mediator would make more sense. Other than wedding gifts, we had mercifully few possessions—none I was really attached to. I got the antique brass bed and the charcoal drawing of the beach in Nantucket. He got the couch, most of the CDs (not a big deal: I have Spotify), our midcentury break-front, and a TV the size of Rhode Island. He stayed in our two-bedroom near Gramercy Park; I moved to my current, smaller place on the Upper West Side. When he wasn't looking, I took the Instant Pot.

I'm thinking of Andrew and our honeymoon—and our divorce—as my mother and I stare at the charred mess that is temporarily Notre Dame. The burnt ruins of the great cathedral are surrounded by scaffolding. It's cordoned off. You can't get within a hundred yards of the place.

"They won't let us inside," my mother says, annoyed. She takes it as a personal affront. "This place was so beautiful. You know, your father and I came here right before I was pregnant with you."

"Really? You never told me that."

"Yes. Kind of like a second honeymoon. I miss him," she says.

Now that's something she's told me many times. Their whole life, they were *thisclose*...with very little room in between for me.

"And the whole fire could have been avoided. That's the saddest part," she says. "They're pretty sure it happened because of human error."

Human error. Like holding a blowtorch the wrong way. Like thinking love will last forever...or at least twenty-five years.

I feel myself welling up with tears. My mother notices.

"Don't cry," she says, trying to console me. "President Macron promises that they'll have it completely restored within five years."

Yeah, right. Another man, another promise.

CHAPTER 8

PÂTÉ EN CROÛTE, RILLETTES of pork. A classic bouillabaisse, the spicy fish soup infused with saffron, orange, and thyme. A couple of glasses of a fruity 2015 Sancerre.

Yes, definitely a four-star meal in a tiny no-star restaurant: Chez Luisa, a simple brasserie across from our hotel.

The food was so good that my mother actually cut me some slack. She didn't even bat an eye when I suggested we order dessert. So we did: dacquoise, a cake stacked with layers of almond and hazelnut meringue and whipped cream, all on a buttery biscuit base.

When we get back to our room an hour later, even night owl Liz is ready to conk out. But first, her inflexible nighttime beauty routine: cleanse, tone, hydrate, exfoliate, apply prescription-strength Retinol serum and La Mer moisturizer—followed by a satiny pink sleep mask.

"We have a lot to do tomorrow," she says from beneath the sleep mask. "*Bonne nuit,* darling."

She is asleep in seconds.

Since I took a four-hour nap after we returned from Notre Dame, I am wide awake. Besides, it's my first night in Paris. I could check my email. I could google interesting tourist sites. I could examine dacquoise recipes. But, hey, this is my first chance to be alone.

I decide to do a little exploring. ASCENSEUR VERS LE BAS. Elevator down.

Small groups of people are sitting in the hotel lobby chatting quietly, their conversations muffled into gentle whispers by the thick gold-colored Aubusson tapestries. A few other people are tapping away on their phones and laptops. I make my way to the bar, a small dark room with bronze mirrors on all four sides, and the alluring name La Feuille de Figuier. The Fig Leaf? Cute. Unlike the elegance of the lobby, this place has a modern vibe to it. Tables with bronze metallic tops. Brushed steel chairs with black cushions. Mercifully, the female bartender and waitress are dressed normally. Not a *fig leaf* in sight.

The bar menu, though, is filled with figs. Fig and anise liqueur. Amaro Fig Bitters. Fig martinis. And to indicate how witty the menu-writer can be, a bartender's favorite called Go Fig Yourself.

I look around the room while I try to decide on my drink order. Paris is a wonderful ongoing movie. Everyone and everything is a scene. An elderly couple a table away is scanning the menu and sharing one pair of reading glasses—kind of sweet, actually. (Andrew used to become fairly annoyed with me when I left my glasses at home.) A handful of youngish women at a table in the rear are laughing it up. My guess is it's a book club on holiday. Two other women drinking champagne are sharing the contents of their shopping bags, *ooh*ing and *aah*ing as if they were looking at bags filled with puppies.

And just to my left, a nice-looking gray-haired man in horn-rimmed glasses is drinking alone. Early fifties, I'd say. He sees me checking the drink menu.

"If you're looking for an authentic fig drink," he says in English, in an accent that sounds British, "might I suggest Figenza." He holds up his glass and tips it toward me. "But I believe it's made in Germany, with figs grown in Greece and Turkey...so it's hardly authentically *French*."

I laugh. But I'm also a bit suspicious. I'm way out of practice, talking to unfamiliar men in hotel bars. Though I do recall a lot of those conversations ending with "Why don't we have a nightcap up in my room?"

I check the menu again and read the description aloud: *Born under the Mediterranean sun, Figenza is a breathtaking masterpiece made with the very finest Mediterranean fruit married with delicately smooth premium vodka. A splendid gift from the angels.* "Sounds good," I tell the bartender.

She pours me a glass over ice. The drink has a nice purplish-green sheen to it, reflecting the colored light above and the copper granite bar top. I take a sip. I like it. I turn to my new friend and say, "Those angels sure knew what they were doing. Cheers."

I raise my glass to him and pretend to clink. He leans over. Our glasses still don't touch. He leans over more, holding onto the bar to support himself. I like that he doesn't automatically slide over to the empty seat between us. So I tap the bar stool a few times. He looks relieved.

"Thank you for that," he says. He switches seats to get closer to me. Now our knees are almost touching. "Might have been a tad awkward if I'd tumbled onto your lap."

"Tad Awkward," I say. "Sounds like the name of a painfully shy stand-up comedian."

He laughs. It is a nice laugh.

"You seem to know your way around the bar menu," I say. "Do you come here often?"

Wait. *Did I really say that?* The oldest pickup line in the book? I'm more out of practice than I thought.

"Hardly. I live in Hackney, East London. And you?"

"New York."

"Ah. The Big Apple." Somehow the cliché sounds way more elegant with his British accent.

I tell him this.

"Actually, I was born in Zimbabwe," he says. "A city called Bulawayo. But my father transferred to London when I was a teenager so I guess I'm a hybrid. I'm Richard Northcott, by the way." Nice name.

"I'm . . . Laurie," I say. My New York reflexes kick in. I can't possibly give him my last name. I was foolishly brave even giving my first name. What if he's an ax murderer?

"I'm here on business," he says. Then adds, "But *you* are here on holiday."

"How can you tell?"

"If it were business, right now you'd be at dinner with a large group of very dull people, discussing marketing shares or algorithms or something equally dreary . . . where at least one in your party will over-indulge, get sozzled, and, uh, start coming on to you."

Sozzled. Great word.

"You're right," I say. "I'm here with my mother." He must see my eyeballs roll.

"Aaah. Say no more."

"She's upstairs now. Although my guess is she still doesn't know I'm gone."

"I gather the old girl is a few sandwiches short of a picnic?"

"What? Oh, no—not at all. But when I left, she was already asleep."

"Mothers," he says. "What is that old adage from years back . . . ?" He thinks for a moment, scrunching his face up. He looks cute when he thinks. Like a little boy. Then he remembers the line. "Ah, yes. The definition of a Freudian slip: *when you say one thing, but you mean a mother*."

I laugh. Yes, I've heard it before. But never with a British accent.

"Well, I'm, uh, alone this time," he says. "And I must say—it's refreshing to have left the children home."

Oh.

"How many children do you have?" I ask.

"Oh, they're not real children. Just a bunch of whiny interns at my law firm. I often bring one or two with me on these trips, but I decided Papa needed some time alone."

He pauses and signals the bartender. "Another one of these, please." He gestures to his glass and then looks at me. She pours him a second glass.

"Ready for another?" he asks.

"I've barely made a dent in this one," I say.

I watch as he takes a sip of his fresh drink. He is clean shaven and smells a bit like patchouli.

"But I must tell you, knowing those young people as I do, I do worry about the entire British legal system," Richard Northcott says.

"So you're an attorney," I say. He smiles.

"Technically, I'm a solicitor." He pauses. "I know

that's, uh, a bit of a naughty word, where you come from."

Am I blushing? Probably. I've watched enough *Law & Orders* to know what it means when a woman is arrested for soliciting.

"What brings you here?"

"A handful of people who witnessed a crime," he says. "And I'm the lucky bloke sent to do the depositions." He takes another sip.

"There are worse places to be stuck," I say.

"Indeed. And I do enjoy just faffing around by myself. I must confess: I spend an excessive amount of time shopping. I'm a sucker for French shoes."

He lifts up his foot to prove it. He's wearing smooth coffee-colored brown leather shoes with laces that are perfectly tied. I wouldn't have thought brown shoes would look good with a gray suit. But I would have been wrong.

"And has Mum been behaving?" he asks.

"Hard to say. It's only Day One."

As we speak, I'm aware of a phenomenon I've noticed several times when I meet a new man: Richard Northcott seems to have actually grown better looking. His blue eyes sparkle a bit brighter. Now when his horned-rimmed glasses slide down his nose, it's no longer annoying. It's absolutely adorable. He even looks younger than I first imagined. A few minutes ago he was early fifties. Now he's easily forty-five.

"So if you're doing depositions…you must speak fluent French," I say.

"Not one whit. Alas, as a young lad I went to one of those hideous schools where they force you to take four years of Latin with a quiz every Tuesday and Friday. No modern language was considered worth studying. What about you?"

"High school French, plus one year in college, where we spent two semesters translating one book line for line. *Vol de Nuit.*"

"Well, I have a thought. Please don't think me cheeky, but…do you think Mum might be willing to share you one afternoon, or would she be miffed?"

"Oh, I'm sure that would be fine."

"Good. I've not got any meetings the day after to-morrow. We could leg it over to a museum or gallery, if that suits you."

"That would be lovely," I say.

"Are you sure? I mean, I don't want to over-egg the pudding here."

I have no idea what that means. But it sounds terrific. "Perhaps you could even teach me a bit of your conversational college French," he adds.

"You mean like, *'Waiter, this soup is too salty,'* and *'Sorry, I thought that was my umbrella'*?"

"Precisely."

"Or how about: *'Do you have these python boots in a size twelve?'*"

Now he really laughs, a big throw-your-head-back laugh. "So it's all settled then. You shall teach me French," he says.

"Yes," I say. "And you will teach me British."

I finish my drink and slide off the stool. A lovely conversation with a lovely man who seems genuinely interested in me, if only for the length of two drinks. But that's fine for now. It's been a while since that happened.

He leans over and kisses me on the cheek. I've left my phone charging in my room, but I give him my number and he saves it in his. Somehow, I make it from the bar all the way up to my room. I don't remember much about the elevator ride. My mind is too full of…joy? Hope? Smiles?

All of the above.

CHAPTER 9

THE JOY IS SHORT-LIVED.

I no sooner put the key in the door and open it than I see my mother sitting up in bed. She's wearing her glasses and reading her favorite magazine, *The International Journal of Gynecology and Obstetrics*. She freezes when she sees me. And then says three words guaranteed to put a damper on the last hour:

"Where...were...you?"

What's very cool about my mother and her implicit criticisms is that she delivers the words gently, a soft conversational tone, one that I assume she uses to calm and help her patients. It is the conversational equivalent of "an iron hand in a velvet glove." Or at least it always sounds that way to me.

Where...were...you?

The same three words she uttered when I was a

teenager, coming home late from a party...or from school...or from anywhere I was having a good time.

I'm tempted to act like a teenager and tell her to *chill, Mother*. But I know that wouldn't go over well with her.

"I couldn't sleep, so I went downstairs to poke around and get a drink," I say.

"I so wish you'd have left a note. That might have prevented me from having a *second* minor heart attack," she says with a smile.

"You were asleep when I left," I say. "Dead to the world."

"Oh, I see."

"Where could I have gone? I left my bag here. My passport. My phone."

"I know. I tried to call you. You've been gone quite a while."

This could easily be the beginning of an unsolvable, unending I'm-a-grown-woman argument. I'm not going to do it. And anyway, my mother has something else she wants to say.

"You met a man, didn't you?"

I try not to roll my eyes. But I can't help myself. This question makes it official: she has supernatural powers.

"Yes, I did. I met a Moroccan prince. I'm flying with him tomorrow to Casablanca, where I will be joining his harem."

"Whatever suits you, darling. After all, it's your life."

I head to the bathroom to change into my nightshirt. When I finish brushing my teeth, I return to say good night. But something is not quite right. My mother is sitting up in bed, hand over her heart, looking like she is going to pledge allegiance. I am about to make a typical wiseass comment.

Then I realize it's something else.

"What's wrong?" I ask.

"Nothing," she says, way too quickly.

"Are you in pain?" I ask.

There is the smallest, tiniest hesitancy between my question and her answer—maybe a second or two. But enough so I am not surprised when she qualifies it: "Well, I wouldn't exactly call it *pain*..."

It's a feeling, she explains. Not quite a fluttering. Nothing that you could probably even measure on a chart.

"It's just...a *sense*," she says.

I am about to ask: *of what*? But then a chill rushes through me. *Her heart.* I brought her here for the sole purpose of giving her something to look forward to after her heart scare. And yet I had no compunction about leaving her alone tonight.

The chill disappears from my body. In its place comes a wave of guilt. *What was I thinking? That's why she was so concerned when I wasn't here.* She knew I was okay. But she was worried about herself.

I walk over to her bed. She's a little pale, but looks okay.

"It's better now," she says. And because I want to believe her, I do.

I make a mental note: *Don't leave her alone again.* No matter how she protests.

Two more mental notes: *Try not to think about Richard Northcott and a possible missed opportunity.* That will be hard.

More important: *Try not to aggravate her.* That will be even harder.

CHAPTER 10

TIME TO WAKE UP.

Time to shine.

Time to say,

"The world is mine."

That song is an original composition. Music and lyrics by Dr. Elizabeth Ormson. Performed by Dr. Elizabeth Ormson. I believe I am the only one who's ever heard it. Approximately two thousand times.

My eyes remain closed. But if I don't show her I'm awake, my mother won't hesitate to do an encore.

"Bonjour, maman," I say.

"I thought you'd be dressed and ready by now."

"No, you didn't," I say. She smiles.

"No, I didn't. But I was so hoping."

Judging by her impatience it must be near noon and we have missed our *petit-déjeuner compris*—our *full breakfast included.* I look at my watch. Oh, for God's sake. It's barely eight.

"How did you sleep?" I ask.

"Very well, once you returned from your carousing. And you?"

"Fine," I say. I don't want to tell her the truth: I tossed and turned for hours, worrying about her, what could happen to her here, and what I should do if something does.

"I've been up for hours," she says, gloating, as if we had a contest and she won.

She looks terrific; it's like last night never happened. She is fully dressed in a champagne-colored pantsuit with a beige silk blouse and cream-colored leather boots. More importantly: she is fully made up. This is no small feat for my mother. Her morning routine is even more elaborate than her evening one: cleansing, toning, vitamin C serum, hyaluronic acid, Chanel moisturizer, La Mer foundation, lipstick, and blush— and about seven layers of sunblock. Watching her get ready on an ordinary day is like watching an actor prepare to go onstage as the Elephant Man.

Yawning, stretching, I get out of bed and head to the bathroom. I turn on the faucet and step into the giant stall shower. The water pressure is strong and exhilarating, like standing under a waterfall. And then my nose kicks in, big time. The bar of soap in the shower is Sisley Eau de Tropical. This was the soap in our honeymoon hotel. I loved the soap so much—and Andrew loved me so much—that he secretly purchased ten bars on the Rue du Faubourg Saint-Honoré and brought them back home to surprise me.

I dry myself with one of the thick white towels folded neatly on a rack, then slip into the terry cloth robe hanging behind the door. Brushing my teeth comes next. My morning ritual is a tad simpler than my mother's. L'Oréal lip gloss and, since I'm in Paris, some eyeliner.

Back in my room, I pull on a pair of black leggings and a white cotton shirt and walk into the sitting room. My mother is thumbing through the room service menu and scowling.

"Too many carbs," she says, to no one in particular. Then she sees me.

"You're all ready?" she asks, looking me up and down. That's Ormson-speak for *"Is that what you're wearing in the chicest city in the world?"*

"Reverse-chic is even chicer," I say.

"Well, then, you'll be the most stunning woman in Paris," she says. "By the way, I've arranged for us to have a private guide today."

"What for?"

"You and I both have been to Paris several times. Rather than wander to the same old places, we can check out some out-of-the-way spots only a native would know. I thought you'd like that."

Actually, I don't.

The last thing I want is someone I don't know dragging me around to places I don't care about, citing statistics I'm not interested in. (*"Paris measures 105 square kilometers with a population of yada yada blah blah blah."*) I'd much rather wander around and discover things on my own. But of course, I'm not in charge.

Then again, it might be good to have a foil. A third person joining us will distract my mother and perhaps take her attention off me.

"What's his name?" I ask.

"Her name. Françoise. Janine recommended her."

"Oh. If *Janine* recommends her..."

I leave the sentence unfinished to see if my mother will pick up on the sarcasm and lob the ball back to me. I can just imagine the little off-the-beaten-path spots a Janine protégé will recommend. Dior. Hermès. The fur department at Le Bon Marché.

"Françoise is a student," my mother says, as if she knows what I'm thinking. "I believe Janine said she's twenty-eight. A lot closer to your age than mine. So she'll probably take us to places *even you* might want to see."

Even me. The slug. The troglodyte.

Her sarcasm is alive and kicking after all. For a moment, I was worried.

CHAPTER 11

WE HEAD DOWN TO breakfast. The restaurant is
paneled in the same mahogany as the check-in desk.
Small tables with starched white tablecloths dot the
room, filled with couples and families and people who
look like they're traveling on business. As each table
empties, the staff begins changing the linens and setting up for lunch. A hostess in a red dress hands
us menus.

"*Bonjour,*" she says with a smile. She is wearing lipstick the exact shade of red as her dress.

"*Bonjour. Comment ça va?*" my mother asks.

"*Bien, merci,*" says the woman. "*Alors, deux personnes?*"
My mother nods her head. Just two of us. Yes.

As we are led to our seats, we pass a buffet table with
all sorts of pastries: biscuits, and sweet sugary *viennois-
erie*. Several raspberry tarts, crème-filled beignets, and
éclairs are arranged in circles, surrounded by dishes of

strawberry, apricot and plum confiture (jam), *le miel* (honey), and thick lemon curd.

"The keto diet would never work here," my size-eight mother says as she sits down and carefully places the cloth napkin on her lap. At the table next to us, a small child is joyously biting into a chocolate croissant, smearing chocolate all over her mouth as her parents laugh and take pictures. All three of them are giggling.

At another table, a bunch of men and women in suits are going over some notes. It looks like a meeting. *Could Richard be here as well?* I look around the room, hoping he is but also dreading the idea of introducing him to my mother.

No sign of him.

A waitress in a black uniform comes to take our order. She's wearing a stiff white apron and a stiff half-smile. It's obvious she would rather be working somewhere else. She pours steaming *café* into our cups.

"Does the granola have dried apricot in it?" my mother asks.

"*Non, madame.* Just nuts and raisins."

"Fine. I'll have a bowl of yogurt with granola."

"*Very good, madame.* And *mademoiselle* desires . . . ?"

Everything, I think. "*La même,*" I say. The same.

"*Bien.*"

The waitress bows slightly, then scurries off to put in our order.

"You know," my mother says in her most serious voice, as if she is addressing a crowd, "the French don't eat eggs for breakfast. They think it's foolish that we do. They feel eggs are a dinner item. I would have ordered poached eggs, but..."

I'm barely listening. I'm watching a young man and woman drinking hot chocolate and eating pieces of baguette dipped in honey. They look like kids. Could they be lovers? No. Most probably brother and sister. But then I see him wipe a dot of honey from her lips. Definitely lovers, and barely out of their teens.

When did twenty start to look so young?

Our yogurt arrives. My mother scoops off half the granola and dumps it on her bread plate before taking her first spoonful. *Watch those calories.*

We eat our granola in silence for a few minutes. "I spoke to Françoise this morning. She wanted to meet us at the Église Saint-Serge, the Russian Orthodox church over on the Rue de Crimée. She said, 'You've never seen anything like it. It's like being in the Russian countryside.' I told her that you and I had both been to Saint-Serge. And if I wanted to be near the Russian countryside, I would have booked a trip to Moscow."

I smile a warm, sincere smile. Andrew and I sent her a postcard from that beautiful church with its colorful painted carvings. She remembered!

"You *have* been there, right, dear?"

Hmmm. Maybe she didn't.

As I've said, the honeymoon was wonderfully romantic. (I've already mentioned the soap.) And Andrew was perfect, as perfect as a husband can be. He had light brown hair. He was respectably tall without being *too* tall. He was California handsome, not in a surfer sort of way but in a Stanford Business School sort of way. (My father was impressed with his career. Even Dr. Liz thought he was charming and handsome.) He worked for a small brokerage firm where he made enough money to buy a two-bedroom *near* but not *on* Gramercy Park. He persisted in helping me with my tennis game until I stopped reflexively breaking my backhand. He was very patient and deliciously slow when it came to sex. And then the day after my birthday dinner at Eleven Madison Park, he emailed me to tell me that he was pretty sure that he was still in love with his former college roommate's wife, a woman who was no longer married to his former college roommate. Let's not dwell on it.

"So Françoise is meeting us here instead," my mother says. "Oh look! That must be her. She looks even younger than I imagined." (Often people don't mean to be irritating; it just happens.)

My mother waves at a young woman who's heading to our table.

Oh, God. It's worse than I thought.

CHAPTER 12

FRANÇOISE COULD BE MY mother's clone.

Blond, frosted hair...champagne-colored sweater and wool slacks...beige booties, and an authentic Louis Vuitton bag slung casually over her shoulder.

Françoise and my mother look like they came out of the same box. Me? I look like I should be helping the waitress serve café au lait.

"Bonjour!" Françoise says. *"Vous êtes les Ormsons?"*

"Ah, oui," my mother says.

"I'm Françoise. So nice to meet you." *Of course, her English is perfect.*

"Please, call me Liz. And this is my daughter, Laurie. Have you had breakfast yet, Françoise?"

"Yes. But please, continue. We can talk about our itinerary as you eat."

"The yogurt here is excellent," my mother says.

"Everything here is excellent," says Françoise. "But, for me, too many carbs."

Too many carbs?

But wait. It gets worse. Not only does she look like my mother, dress like my mother, and think like my mother...she isn't just a student.

"Janine tells me you go to school," my mother says. "What are you studying?"

"I'm at the Descartes University Medical School."

Of course she is. Okay, that's it. Where's the carafe with the café au lait?

I dig into the rest of my yogurt, now lusting more than ever after the pastries across the room.

"Janine also told me a bit about *you*," Françoise says. "But I'd like to know more about your tastes. What kinds of things would you like to see? Architecture? Historical sites? I assume you've already seen the major museums."

As Françoise tells us about some of the lesser-known places we could explore, I realize that they fall into two basic categories: landmarks and science.

"Are there any off-the-beaten-track art museums you might recommend?" I ask.

"There is one you would love," she says. "The Musée Jacquemart-André. Edouard André and Nélie Jacquemart were a French power couple who amassed one of Europe's most impressive private art collections. Not unlike the Frick Museum in New York City."

"Perfect," I say.

As we head to our first hidden treasure attraction, the Catacombs, my mother and Françoise walk together, practically hand in hand. I bring up the rear. They get into a lively discussion about Françoise's future plans. She is thinking about obstetrics, but also neurology. She was a chemistry major at the Sorbonne. She is also considering genetic research.

That clinches it. Without a doubt, this woman is definitely The Daughter My Mother Always Wanted.

The Catacombs, Françoise tells us, is a resting place for bones. "It's also known as an ossuary."

Nice word, I think. But not as nice as *sozzled* or *cheeky*.

As soon as we pay our admission fee, it starts. Drum-roll, please, because . . . Here Come the Statistics!

Begun in 1780! . . .

The bones of over 6 million people! . . .

320 kilometers of tunnels! . . .

I have to admit, I'm being unfair. That's what happens when you're very, very insecure in a relationship: me and my mother, me and Andrew, me and pretty much everybody outside of the office (the one place where I pretty much know what I'm doing). The slightest thing can set off a wave of anxiety and self-doubt.

The Catacombs are actually the perfect hidden-treasure attraction for the two of us. My mother is fascinated by the science of it (cemeteries were over-crowded and overflowing, causing disease—so the bones were dug up and transferred to an abandoned underground labyrinth). And I'm intrigued by the art, how since the eighteenth century, various artisans have used bones to make macabre but beautiful sculptures, heart and circle designs.

Several Hidden Treasures later—the Petite Ceinture, an abandoned railway line; Gustave Eiffel's secret apartment in the tower; remnants of a Paris guillotine—Françoise consults her list. We have time for one more stop.

It's a choice between the museum she mentioned earlier, the Musée Jacquemart-André, or the best off-the-beaten-path shopping area in all of Paris.

Sorry, Edouard and Nélie. Your private art collection doesn't stand a chance.

We are about to hop into a cab and head to the shops when my mother spots something that makes her stop in her tracks.

"Look!" she says, pointing to a poster hanging on an iron Art Nouveau streetlamp.

It's the only thing that could distract her from an afternoon of boutique-hopping.

CHAPTER 13

MINUTES LATER, THE THREE of us are standing in the lobby of the Musée des Arts Décoratifs. Our final— entirely unplanned—Hidden Treasure of the Day.

My mother is buying a ticket to an exhibit of antique Cartier jewelry from the nineteenth and twentieth centuries: a gallery of precious gems, artistically exhibited to look like they're in natural habitats. Lobby photos of the exhibit show coral rings and necklaces hanging from fishing nets. Diamond bracelets and brooches are strung up like glittery constellations, suspended from a navy-blue velvet night sky. The Duchess of Windsor's famous sapphire-and-diamond panther brooch crouches in a make-believe green silk jungle.

It's a dazzling display of priceless gems, none of which my mother can afford, but all of which she believes she's entitled to.

Ticket in hand, she waves goodbye and darts inside. I don't think I've ever seen her move so fast. Her last words to us: "I'm sure you two can find something to keep you busy for an hour or so." Then she disappears.

Françoise and I head to a nearby café filled with French workmen, all smoking Gauloises and arguing. We plop ourselves down onto the last two remaining seats. Correction: I plop down. Françoise seats herself carefully, tucking the hem of her knee-length, champagne-colored cardigan beneath her.

I am about to order a glass of Sancerre, but Françoise orders a bottle.

I don't usually drink this early in the afternoon, but what the heck. As they say, *When in Rome…*

Then I also ask for a *mousse au chocolat* sprinkled with *sucre en poudre*—hoping that What Happens with Françoise, Stays with Françoise.

"Tell me about your work," she says. So I do: a five-minute, condensed survey class of Advertising 101. I tell her about accounts, clients, commercial shoots all over the world, and postproduction when you're hunched over editing machines or sitting in recording studios.

She seems fascinated.

"As a doctor, you see the same thing over and over and over," she says. "But what *you* do—that all sounds so interesting."

"Well maybe, but doctors are saving lives. What am I saving? Rice Krispies? Cheez Whiz?"

"Still," she says, "You come from a much more color-ful world than I do. I hope this little tour was not too boring for you."

"Not at all," I say. I really mean it. Françoise is intelligent and fun. By the end of our first glass of wine, we have gotten through the basic "first-date questions": she's twenty-eight, from Marseille, living with a room-mate she only moderately gets along with because the woman is such a *plouc*—a slob. (Like most things, it sounds classier in French.)

By the start of our second glass of wine, I feel like I'm with a girlfriend. So of course, we indulge in some girl talk. In other words: we talk about boys. Men.

"I recently ended an engagement," she says. She seems a little sad but not heartbroken. "Arnaud was everything my family wanted for me: rich, successful, devoted. And," she adds, "faithful."

Well, that's where the comparisons to Andrew end.

"Our parents were best friends. It was always as-sumed we'd be married some day. But..." She pauses to search for the right words. "What can I say? There was no magic. I knew him my whole life. He was always just *there*. Like...like..."

"Furniture?" I ask.

"Exactly! Like a comfy chair," she says and laughs. Then she gets serious again. "He gave me a beautiful diamond."

"My mother would approve of that."

"When I broke off the engagement, I wanted to give it back. It had been his grandmother's. But he insisted I keep it. I think because...can I be totally honest?"

I don't just say yes. I raise my glass to toast her.

"I think he was relieved," she says. "He didn't want to marry me, either. It was just something he thought he was supposed to do."

An attractive man nearby is looking at Françoise as she gestures and laughs. She doesn't seem to notice.

Since Arnaud, there have been other men in her life. But still no magic. And she's *très confortable* being single, no matter what her parents think.

My turn to tell her about Andrew. How I thought we were happy. How shocked I was when he pulled the rug out from under me and revealed he was still smitten with a woman he dated before me.

"How did your mother take that?"

Ah, interesting question.

"My mother is the survivor of a very happy marriage," I tell her. "Thirty-seven years of bliss. She was devoted to my father. And he doted on her. And then there was me—popping up in their lives like one of those buoys you find at sea."

I realize I am about to veer into one of my woe-is-me sagas. Better to save that for my weekly sessions with Esther. So I get back on track.

"So she was...very, very sad. She liked Andrew. More importantly, she approved of him. So I felt like I had disappointed her, big time. Somehow, I had picked the wrong man."

"But you say she approved of him."

"Yes."

How do I explain to my new friend that it's often what my mother doesn't say that's more powerful than what she does say?

Two small glasses of wine, midday, have given me enough of a buzz to decline a third. There's half a bottle left. Françoise pours herself a third glass. I push the bottle over to her side, so she can have the last glass as well.

"Let me ask you something," I say, polishing off my chocolate mousse. "All those stories we hear about French men having mistresses on the side . . ."

"While their wives look away? No," she says, shaking her head. Then she asks, "Would *you* have looked away if you knew what Andrew was up to?"

Even just thinking about the answer makes my stomach hurt.

"Maybe some fabulously wealthy men can get away with it," she says. "But in today's climate? When mistresses are convinced they have rights, or even lawsuits? No. It's just too risky. French marriages are as good or as rocky as any others."

We see my mother waving to us from across the street.

"So that's my story," Françoise says, wrapping up the saga of Arnaud. "Bottom line: Two great old French families did *not* get united in marriage."

"But two great French people—Arnaud and you—became wiser for it," I say.

"Yes. Thank you, Laurie," she says, toasting me with her last sip. "I really needed to hear that. My life is filled with people who are still on his side."

I've decided Françoise is a lovely person. It's not her fault that she's thinner than I am.

CHAPTER 14

FRANÇOISE WAS RIGHT: WHEN tourists flock to the 17th arrondissement, it's to see the Eiffel Tower. They don't realize that just a few blocks away is the Rue Saint-Dominique, one of the classiest streets in all of Paris. Shop after shop of very cool French clothing brands reeking of chic elegance but with a modern vibe. The shoppers are all Parisian. Not a tourist in sight.

Did I mention that my mother is the real shopper here? Me, I'm just keeping her company. Dr. Liz shows her stuff at our first stop, Comptoir des Cotonniers. I stand on the side and watch her try on a series of navy-blue blazers that bear a striking resemblance to all her other navy blazers, except for the gold French buttons. Meanwhile, she's chatting with one of the salesgirls. At one point, the salesgirl—I should properly call her *la vendeuse* in a place this fancy—throws her head back in raucous laughter.

Wait a minute. Is my mother funny? She's never been funny before. Maybe she's just funny in French.

I stand there killing time until something occurs to me: *if* I hear from Richard Northcott, and *if* he wants to see me, and *if* I get the go-ahead from my mother...I have nothing to wear. Practically all I've brought to Paris are jeans, black leggings, and a couple of simple blouses—what the pundits refer to as *business casual,* and my mother refers to as *business lazy.*

I look around the shop. Lots of silk skirts and shirts to mix and match. Classic, I guess, but also dreary. Then something on a mannequin catches my eye: a simple black knit dress. It's jersey, but not the super-clingy type—maybe some sort of rayon blend. Long sleeves, with a V-neck that stops just above the cleavage. Somewhat sexy, but not outrageously so. A dress with definite possibilities.

I rummage through the rack until I find it in my size. I carry it to the dressing room and strip down to my bra and panties. I am just about to slip into it when the curtain is yanked open.

"Hey!" I yell, startled, throwing my arms around my breasts. But it's just the *vendeuse,* followed closely by *ma mère.* The salesgirl eyes the dress I am about to try on and shakes her head no.

"*Vous devez enlever votre soutien-gorge,*" she says. I don't get it.

She points to the dress. *"Cette robe doit être sans soutien-gorge."*

I still don't get it.

"She wants you to take off your bra," my mother says.

What? No!

"In front of you two? *Pourquoi?*" I ask her. *Why?*

Big mistake. She answers in French.

"C'est comme il est censé être porté."

"For God's sake," my mother says. "This is Paris. She's seen breasts before."

"Yes. But not *mine*."

Torn between embarrassment and anger, and completely outnumbered, I unhook my bra and hand it to my mother. Then I pull the dress on. I see what they mean; the dress has darts around the bust and mesh cups inside designed to shape and support the breasts without any seams or straps showing.

"I like this," I say. My mother nods her head in agreement. "And it will probably be good to have a dress like this, if the man from the bar wants to take me to dinner."

My mother's face shifts from smile to frown. She opens her mouth as if she's going to say something. Then, just as quickly, she changes her mind.

Now that she's seen me practically naked, the salesgirl introduces herself. Her name is Gabrielle. More than *une vendeuse,* she is a fashion consultant. Fashion by intimidation. Typical of the French.

But we all agree: the dress is quite flattering. My mother says something to her in French. Gabrielle nods *oui* and smiles.

"What did you say to her?"

"I said how slenderizing it is."

Gabrielle weighs about eighty pounds. I wonder if she even knows what slenderizing means.

Armed with my new dress, we make a second stop: Claudie Pierlot. If Comptoir is classic, Claudie Pierlot is just the opposite. I see tons of short skirts and sexy "cold-shoulder" necklines. Lots of bright halter tops that stop at the navel, paired with black leather motor-cycle jackets. There's a display of fuzzy fur clutch bags on my left. And an entire aisle filled with sky-high heels in unexpected rainbow colors like purple and chartreuse.

The store is filled with shoppers. And not one of them is over eighteen.

"This would look nice on you," my mother says. She's holding up a comfy-looking gray sweater, prob-ably cashmere. At first, I think she might be right.

But as she hands it to me, I see the front is covered with sparkling beads and sequins in the shape of a unicorn. Not my style. I shake my head no; my mother frowns. Agreeing so easily on that black dress was a once-in-a-lifetime experience. But now we are about to go into our usual mother-daughter shopping mode. You'd think, after all these years, I'd be used to this.

Or that I'd have the brains to wait outside while my mother shops her little heart out.

Yeah. You'd think.

Sandro is shop number three. Simple functional clothing, but with simply ridiculous prices. Not a problem. I've done my shopping for the day. I sit down in a leather chair and watch my mother. She's made a beeline for a sleeveless hot-pink dress with cut-out designs. Definitely elegant. Definitely uber-trendy. I'm sure she'll look great in it. She looks great in everything.

"Come with me," she says, heading to the dressing room. "Here," she says, handing me the dress. "Try this on."

Say what? Pink? Knee-length? Sleeveless? *Me?*

She eyes me up and down. "I don't understand it," she says. "You're a beautiful young woman. Are you afraid if you wear pink instead of black, someone might notice you?"

I'm a *what*? Can we roll back the tape? *Beautiful. Young. Woman.* I've heard her use those words before, many times. Just never in reference to me.

"Do you really think that?" I ask.

"That you like to disappear? Absolutely."

"No, I mean...you think I'm...beautiful?"

"Of course I think that. If only *you* thought so, too."

There's an undercurrent of exasperation in my mother's comment, but I don't hear it. Dr. Liz Ormson, whose patients are actresses, society women, and super-models, thinks I'm *beautiful*?

The enormity of that one word is so deep, I don't know where to process it. My brain? My heart? My gut?

As a way of saying thanks, I try on the pink dress. As expected, I look like a horse in a circus parade. It is clearly made for a young teenager.

"No. I was wrong. It's not for you," she says. She's disappointed. But I'm not.

I may not be the ruffles or lace or flirty cut-out type. But my mother thinks I'm beautiful.

If only she had mentioned that twenty years ago.

CHAPTER 15

"MOTHER, I JUST STRANGLED the chambermaid."

You'd think that's what I just confessed, based on the look of sheer horror on my mother's face.

What I actually said was, "Mother, I can't find my passport."

"What do you mean, you can't find it?"

"I put it in my bag, right here. But now..."

"Obviously you did *not* put it there or it would still be there," she says. She always was a stickler for logic. And of course, she's right. But still.

Piece by piece, I pull everything out of my duffel bag and put it on the bed. My leggings. My jeans. My bras. My slippers. My shirts.

It's not in any of my zippered pockets. My makeup case. My jewelry case.

Last but not least: a small plastic bag of condoms, just in case I meet a dreamy guy with an STI. Ordinarily

Liz Ormson would have something to say about that. But she lets it slide.

"Could I have left it at the airport?"

"No," she reminds me. "We had to show them at the desk when we checked in."

She goes to the room safe and clicks it open with the password she selected: my father's birth date.

"You didn't put your passport in here, either," she says. Of course, she adds, "Like *I* did."

She appears to be waiting impatiently while I pull apart everything I own—zippers, pockets, flaps. But I know the signs: the tap-tapping of her nails on the desk. The sighs masquerading as deep breaths. She is about to go off on a tear and say something both of us will regret.

"I do have a copy of it," I say, pulling out a wrinkled Xerox. If I thought she would be impressed by that, I am mistaken. I grab my phone and look up the address and hours of the American embassy. "It's Sunday. They're closed today. But it opens at nine tomorrow morning."

"I hope you won't need it for anything *today*," she says.

"I won't. Not unless I decide to flee the country." Which is looking better and better as her anger grows.

Then she gets an idea.

She goes into the bathroom and gets one of the clean glasses, rips off the sanitized paper top, and puts the glass upside down on the desk.

"What's that for?" I ask.

"It's an old Jewish superstition. If you lose something, put a glass upside down. Whatever you lost will soon turn up."

She seems so sure of this, I choose not to remind her that (1) she's not superstitious and (2) she's not Jewish.

"Where did you hear about that?" I ask instead.

"Your father's mother."

"Grandma Miriam?"

"Yes."

Grandma Miriam has been dead for twenty years. I never heard of this before. But Dr. Liz is always full of surprises.

Anyway, it's late. We've had a great but exhausting day. So exhausting, we decided to stay in and order room service (poached eggs and a salad for her, a burger and an Orangina for me). And now it's time to read a little before bed.

My mother is in the bathroom, creaming and uncreaming her face. I open the book I'm reading, and lo and behold, there it is: my passport. Being used as a bookmark.

"I found it!" I yell out.

"See? I told you that glass trick would work."

CHAPTER 16

I'M LIKE A FOURTEEN-YEAR-OLD who's been sitting by the phone, waiting for the cute guy in my math class to call me. An entire day has gone by. No Richard Northcott yet. And then...the phone rings.

I see I have a text from Drew, my boss, asking me to call him when I have a minute. But I'm more focused on the unfamiliar number calling *me*. A UK number. I answer.

A voice says: "You have bewitched me, body and soul, and I love, I love, I love you."

"...Hello?"

"Laurie? It's, um, it's Richard, from the other night at the bar. And that—that was from *Pride and Prejudice*, the movie version starring Matthew Macfadyen as Mr. Darcy. Did it seem too over the top? I'm sorry. I wanted to make you laugh..."

"You did," I say. I must admit, all the adolescent joy

and excitement I thought I had outgrown bubble up once again as I talk to him. He is even more charming than I remembered.

"Such a nice bit of kismet, meeting you like that," he says.

"Yes," I say, somewhat tongue-tied and self-conscious. Exactly how I was at fourteen. Next thing you know, I'll be using the word *awesome*.

He cuts to the chase. "I was wondering... it's such a grand day. Could I interest you in a bit of a stroll?"

A bit of a stroll? How quaint.

I look over at my mother, who is sitting on the bed, polishing her nails the same Revlon Rubies in the Snow red she has used for a hundred years.

"That would be lovely," I say.

Richard and I agree to meet in the hotel lobby in an hour. I would say I'm walking on the proverbial clouds, except as I hang up, I see a storm on the horizon. A dark cloud who, at this very moment, is waving her hands so her polish will dry.

"Was that Françoise?" she asks. I think quickly. I could say I'm meeting Françoise. But I am the world's worst liar. My mother would see through me in an instant.

"Actually, no. It was Richard. The man I met the other night at the bar."

She looks up quickly. I try to read her expression: Fear? Anger? Disapproval? All of the above?

"Laurenne," she says, using the name on my birth certificate—a dead giveaway that she is about to say something important. "Do you think that's really wise?"

"I'm meeting him in broad daylight. There will be thousands of other people milling around. So if he tries to throw me into his white van . . ."

I wonder if she'll get the reference. She does.

"I don't worry about you being kidnapped," she says. It looks like she's about to say something else, but then changes her mind. No matter. With my mother the subject is never truly closed.

It's Monday morning. We have purposely not planned anything for today after yesterday's hectic schedule. I head to the bathroom to shower. After, I decide to go a little more Liz than Laurie with my makeup. Now's the perfect time to dip into my case of Boujee Cosmetics, courtesy of my new seventy-million-dollar client. I pull out their Rainy Day moisturizer, Deep Dusk eye shadow, Smokestack Black liner, tinted SPF foundation, and Flip Gloss (cute container). I even try my hand at a little sculpting to make my cheekbones pop. The result is . . . not terrible. I smile at myself in the bathroom mirror. Perhaps even Dr. Liz will approve.

She does.

"Now you look like a human being," she says. Ah, the compliments do fly.

Next up: what to wear. A simple walk does not qualify as a New Black Dress event. Instead, I pull on a pair of black leggings with my best black blouse—silk, with a plunging-but-not-too-plunging neckline that re-veals about one quarter of an inch of lace on my purple Lilyette bra. It's definitely a come-hither look, as they say, even though my mother would probably prefer I wear something brighter. But I'm doing it for me as well as for him. After all, I'm a divorcée in the City of Love. Even if nothing comes of it, it's good to feel sexy again.

Now that she sees what I'm wearing, my mother is even more against my going.

I'm not sure if it's the plunging neckline or if she's anxious about being left alone. I must admit, I'm a little concerned about that as well. I know I said I'd never do that again. But it's just a quick stroll. With a lovely man. I'll be back in no time.

"I'll have my cell phone," I say. I'm standing in front of the full-length mirror, doing my hair with my combination blow dryer/curler. "So you can always reach me if—"

"I'm perfectly capable of calling the front desk if I need assistance," she says. "Don't forget. I speak impeccable French."

So why…? "Mother, what exactly are you worried about?"

Still dressed in her elegant Japanese kimono-style bathrobe, she turns to face me.

"I want to tell you a story," she says. "On my first

trip to Paris—I was quite a bit younger than you—twenty-one, I think. It was my senior year of college and we were on spring break. I was with my friend Cecily. Cecily had relatives here, so we stayed with them. A lovely couple with a flat somewhere on the Left Bank."

Cecily. That's a new name. Hmmm. Where's this story going?

"Cecily and I wandered all over the city together. One day when we were looking at prints at one of the kiosks near the river, I started to chat with a young man who worked there. His name was Sacha. He was cute. A few inches taller than me. Not quite the rough-and-tumble sort. But not like any of the college men I knew."

I am all ears.

"He was quite appealing," she says, smiling. "Very French and very well put together, as only the French can be when they have no money. He owned one fabulous yellow knit sweater which he wore . . ." she pauses. "Each time I saw him."

Each time? This is getting interesting.

"He asked me to meet him for coffee, which I did. For the next two days I brought coffee to him at the kiosk and we sat there together all afternoon. He was funny and charming with all the tourists who stopped by, offering his opinions on the prints. He was an artist, you see. So he knew about style and technique, and the difference between prints and lithographs. I was...impressed."

But I'm not twenty-one, I want to say. *I'm thirty-six. And I've been married.* If she thinks anything she tells me is going to stop me—

"Then we went out to dinner one night."

"And I bet it was wonderful," I say. She doesn't notice the sarcasm in my voice.

"No. The dinner was absolutely terrible. I didn't think it was possible to get a bad meal in Paris. How wrong I was! Some sort of grisly stew. Too much garlic. But of course, I was young. It all seemed so romantic back then—a starving artist, a cheap French restaurant. And then at one point, he leaned over and...kissed me."

She looks away. Her words hang so heavy in the air, it's as if I can see them.

"He wanted me to go back to his apartment. At first I declined. But then I thought, 'Why not? I'm in Paris. When will this moment happen again?'"

I must be staring at her.

"Oh, don't look at me that way. You didn't think your father was my very first, did you?"

Now I am glued to her. I can't wait to hear how this ends.

"So I went with him. And, oh, such a dreadful apartment! A fourth-floor walk-up in a dirty area of the Marais. The whole place smelled like cats."

"How many cats did he have?"

"None. That's what made it worse. The cat smell was from the previous tenant. He never even cleaned the place when he moved in."

I know she wants to tell me more. I look at the clock. Still ten minutes before I have to meet Richard.

"And we made love. It was...well, it was my very first time."

This is riveting new information. She's never opened up to me like this before. Maybe that's the power of traveling. If I learn nothing else about my mother in Paris, this alone was worth the trip.

"Oh, don't look so shocked, Laurie. People had sex in those days, too."

I don't know which is more shocking: that Dr. Liz had premarital sex in a walk-up flat in Paris...or that she had *no* sex until her senior year of college.

"He knew I was a virgin, so he took extra time with me. He was quite gentle. Although, of course, I didn't enjoy it at all. And I bled."

Whoa. I should have left the room a sentence or two ago. I think we've verged into TMI territory. Too Much Information.

"What happened when you saw him next?"

"That's the point," she says, as gently as she has ever said anything to me, ever. "I never saw him again. We were supposed to meet up in a café the next afternoon. I waited and waited—and he never showed. I went around to the kiosks, and he wasn't there that day or the day after. And then..."

"What?"

"Then Cecily and I flew home. At first, I was deeply distressed. I'd had such fantasies. And as you know, I am not a person who fantasizes a lot."

Yeah. Tell me about it.

"You see, I had created my own make-believe agenda. That first morning, after being with him the night before, I decided I wasn't going back to America. I was going to stay in Paris and get a job in a little bookstore or something so Sacha and I could get a better apartment and..."

She kept on talking. But I was too shocked to listen. My mother, not going to medical school? Not meeting my father? *Not having me?*

"But once my eyes were opened, I blamed my-self. What did I expect? I was hurt, yes—but as time went on, I realized I had dodged a bullet. Everything important that ever happened to me happened *after* I knew Sacha. I was probably in love with him that one night...but fortunately it never amounted to anything except some nice memories."

"And you're telling me this now because—"

"Because I don't want you to be hurt. This is the City of Love. You're vulnerable. We don't know anything about this man."

"Mother, we're just going for a walk."

"Don't kid yourself," she tells me. "I see how you usually do your makeup. You didn't put all that on *just for a walk*."

Amazing. In one fell swoop—with one simple sentence—my mother is able to compliment me...*and* tear me down.

CHAPTER 17

I HEAD DOWN TO the lobby. Richard is waiting there.
I hope daylight is as kind to me as it is to him. He's
even more handsome than I remember, much closer
to midforties than my original estimate. With those
twinkly blue eyes and boyish smile, he reminds me of
Hugh Grant. Richard is wearing a black leather jacket,
a black shirt, and jeans. Super cool. Super hip. Super
kiss on the cheek when he sees me.

He looks me up and down and seems to like what
he sees.

"So, how are things with Mum?" he asks.

"Not terrible," I say. It's the truth. The story she just
told me verges on a conversation two girlfriends might
have. So there is a little extra spring in my step, even
though I've chosen to wear my black leather Stuart
Weitzman ankle boots with the three-inch heels. *Très
chic,* but not *très confortable.*

"And how are things going on the legal front?" I ask.

"Quite well," he says. "I had allowed four days for it and, uh, it took barely two. Glad you were available on a moment's notice."

"Me, too," I say.

Richard and I are strangers, but I feel very comfortable with him. He gives off a nice, accessible vibe. Maybe I'm just comparing him to the other men I've met recently (in a word: none), or my last encounters with Andrew (as brutal as any televised WWE event).

"It's a tad late in the season for the Luxembourg Gardens," he says. "And I assume, as a New Yorker, you're not much of a gardener anyway."

"True," I say. "My favorite flowers come twelve at a time, in a long white box."

I decide not to add *with a mushy love note attached*. I don't feel *that* comfortable.

"So a simple stroll along the Seine..."

"Would be perfect," I say.

It's a crisp October Monday morning. Dozens of Parisians walk past us: matrons with baguettes sticking out of their string shopping bags. Men of all ages with varying degrees of facial hair. Elegant women walking elegant dogs in elegant rhinestone-studded collars, and a smattering of young parents with toddlers. The rich, the poor, the in-between. All of them so used to Paris that they walk quickly, barely noticing how every street is like a picture postcard.

We walk along the Seine and head north on the pedestrian walkway. The Seine, in all its glory, seems to change every time you blink. Right now, it is gunmetal gray with glints of sunlight. A moment later, a small white sailboat causes it to ripple with tiny white waves.

Then a *bateau mouche*—a ferry loaded with tourists and their cameras—passes, and the water gets rougher and whiter. The tourists wave to us. I wave back. As we pass one of the Seine's many bridges, the Pont d'Arcole, an elderly man on a bicycle loaded with bouquets of irises, jonquils, lilies, and roses narrowly misses us. Richard pulls me to the side just in time. As the man passes, he screams what are probably a dozen French curses. But even that sounds charming.

"You realize," I say, "there's an old Chinese proverb: once you save someone's life, you're responsible for it from then on."

"Oh, dear," Richard says. "That's quite the burden. But do tell: what sort of life do you lead when you're not here?"

"I'm in advertising," I say. "I work at Vanessa, a small agency. Hmmm. I just remembered. I got a text from the executive creative director early this morning asking me to call in quickly. Mind if I do it now?"

"Not at all."

I pull out my cell phone and quickly punch in the international code and Drew's number.

"Laurie!" Drew answers. "Hey—sorry to interrupt your vacation. How's Paris?"

"Well, the good thing is, Parisian elegance trumps maternal aggravation."

"Glad to hear it," he says. "Listen: the Boujee people want us to put together a schedule. I realize this is the last thing on your mind now, but we were wondering…when might we be able to show them some creative ideas? When are you back again?"

Oh, right. I'll have to go back home at some point.

"I'm back on the eighteenth. We're here a few more days, then we hightail it to Norway."

"Norway? Why?"

"That was the whole point of the trip, till my mother snuck Paris in at the last minute."

"No sympathy here, hon," Drew says.

"Yeah. I know. But back to scheduling. I'll take a look at what the creative folks have done the day I'm back."

"And the teams you want on this should be…?"

"Nick and Christine. Also, Alex and Nicole. And if she's not too busy, maybe Joanne could jump in as well."

"Done," Drew says. "So we'll plan on a presentation for the week after that?"

"Sounds reasonable. Email me all the meeting reports I've missed, and I'll read them tonight."

"You sure? I'd hate to get on Dr. Liz's bad side."

Need I add, Drew has met my mother. Many times.

"I'm sure. Take care."

"You too," he says, and we hang up.

"Right before I left, we landed a new client. Boujee Cosmetics," I explain to Richard.

"*Boujee?*" he asks with a wry smile.

I never thought it was a funny name...till now. I try not to laugh as I continue. "I was in charge of the pitch. Anyway, they liked what they saw—"

"I'm not surprised," he says, looking at me. Oh, God. Tell me I'm not blushing...

"And now I'll probably be made creative director on the account."

"Which means?"

"Well, have you watched *Mad Men*? I get involved in strategic directions, then give out the assignments, wait a few days to see what the group comes up with, fend off all arguments from them for why I'm wrong if I ask for revisions...and, in case the client doesn't like what we recommend and is unhappy, everyone at the agency blames me."

"Sounds like my relationship with the interns."

"My leaving when I did could have caused a bit of a headache," I say, "but I did it for my mother's benefit."

"I get it," he says. "Dutiful daughter."

Then I say, "Is your mother...?" I pause.

"Still alive? Yes," he says. "Living on her own and

quite happy in a sweet little bedsit about twenty miles from me. Close enough that I can pop by regularly, but far enough that I can make excuses. Uh-oh," he says suddenly, putting his hand out. "Did you feel something?"

I look up. Those beautiful blue skies have turned the same shade of gray as the Seine. I feel a few raindrops on my head. Neither one of us has an umbrella. People begin scurrying around, covering their heads with whatever's handy—a newspaper, a shopping basket. They duck under canopies and into storefronts.

I assume we will duck into one as well. But it seems Richard has a better idea.

He takes my arm and tells me what he has in mind. And since he's doing the leading, I absolutely, positively, cannot feel guilty for what lies ahead.

CHAPTER 18

NO, IT'S NOT A HOTEL.

It's Ladurée on the Rue Royale. Not just a *pâtisserie*. A little jewel box of sweets. If Hansel and Gretel had been adults, this would have been the candy cottage that sealed their doom.

As we walk in, I spy trays of macarons in every color of the rainbow. We pass racks of gorgeous pastries loaded with fruits and creams. And endless layers of homemade chocolates running the entire length of the shop.

We grab a table. Both of us are drenched from our eight-block walk in the rain. Richard leans over and uses his handkerchief to wipe the water still dripping down my face. Very sweet.

"What shall we order?" he asks.

"Anything," I say. "As long as it's very, very chocolaty."

I watch him as he walks to the counter. I see his

jeans are the very expensive kind, the kind you send out to be dry-cleaned and pressed. Obviously a man who cares how he looks.

The young woman behind the counter has a ton of thick black hair pinned up. She has some sort of hat that looks like a paper cup on her head. Still, she looks like a French Penelope Cruz. Full lips. Green eyes. Even a drab white apron can't take away from her youth and beauty. So it delights me to see that Richard barely looks at her as he points to some pastries under the glass.

He comes back with three pastries. An embarrassment of riches.

"An Ispahan," he says, pointing to the first. "A pink macaron with rose-scented cream, raspberries, and lychees. This second one is a Black Fruit Pavlova—a biscuit infused with lime, panna cotta crème, and seasonal fruits."

He begins to cut them both in half.

"And this last one has an odd name," he says, as he slices it in two. "It's called a Religieuse."

I look at it. Odd name, indeed. A small ball of pink pastry sitting on top of a large ball of pink pastry, with some buttercream frosting in between. It looks like a pink snowman.

"They say it was invented by Catherine de' Medici's Italian chef, who thought it looked like the papal hat. Although the name actually translates to the word *nun*."

Nothing chocolate yet. *Did he forget?*

Then he gets up and goes to the counter, and comes back with two cups. I assume it's coffee. I'm wrong.

"Ta-da! The best hot chocolate in all of Paris," he says. "Perhaps in all of the world."

I take a sip. It's like drinking a hundred chocolate truffles smushed together and topped with whipped cream. Divine and sinful at the same time. And just to make sure it's rich enough, there's a chocolate macaron on the saucer.

"I was going to ask if you had any hobbies," I say. "But I'm starting to realize..."

"That my hobby is food? Guilty as charged. Been cooking since I was seventeen. Mum never let me get anywhere near her kitchen. So of course, I desperately wanted to be there. Started to cook when I went to university...and never stopped."

"Bet she's glad she didn't forbid you from watching porn."

He throws his head back and laughs. "Spot on!" he says, sliding three halves onto my plate.

I taste each. They are all wonderful.

"Do you cook?" he asks.

"Not if I can help it. I've always been the designated eater," I say. "What do you like best about cooking? I mean, besides the end result."

"Hmm. I suppose I would say *the process*. It's like magic. Put a bunch of things together and poof, they turn into something else. Quite Merlin-like, I think."

"Yes. I get that."

"And, of course, having people appreciate it. If there's one thing that really turns me on, it's, uh, satisfying people."

His last words hang in the air between us like a cartoon talk balloon. Okay. Let's face it, he probably meant that in the most innocent way possible. *Or not.* In my frame of mind—a single woman out with a man I find attractive—I begin to blush. And when he sees that, he begins to blush, too.

Fortunately, the shop is suddenly crowded. Several of the "doorway" people have moved inside and are queuing up at the pastry counter. Three young men in muddy soccer uniforms enter. Two of them are checking out the pastries. The third is checking out two young women at the other end of the store. The girls notice him and begin to giggle. Soon all three men wander over to the women and they begin to chat and giggle together. That's *so* Paris.

As the clouds pass and the rain stops, the people begin to disperse. The young soccer players and the girls leave the pastry shop together, headed God knows where.

"Shall we continue our stroll?" Richard asks.

"Absolutely," I say. I'm glad the rain has stopped. If I consume any more sweets, I don't think I could fit under an umbrella.

As we walk along the quay, I take Richard's arm. It

seems like the most natural thing in the world. When I see a billboard for a French cosmetics company with both women and men applying their products, I make a mental note of it. So outré. So, well, French. Maybe something like that could work for Boujee?

But I don't want to think about work now. I focus on the scene all around me. Mothers with rain-dappled strollers are back to pushing their babies. People zig and zag around us on their bikes. Several old men are wiping off wet seats at outdoor cafés, so they can continue their smoking and arguing. And the Seine looks as silvery as ever. It's as if the rain never happened.

Richard looks at me and we smile at each other. I feel . . . *content* is the right word.

But then I suddenly realize where we're heading.

CHAPTER 19

THE PONT DES ARTS. I've read about this Parisian site so many times in my old hard-copy guidebook, I actually memorized it.

A nine-arch metal bridge built for pedestrians back in the 1800s when Napoleon was emperor. It was designed to resemble a hanging garden, with benches and flowers all along the way. Of all the bridges, the Pont des Arts is known as the most romantic.

So it's no surprise that in 2008, one young couple decided to inscribe their names on a lock, hang it on one of the side grates, and throw the key into the Seine. Another couple followed suit. Soon, the bridge became the go-to destination for couples visiting from all over the world.

Including Andrew and me.

We'd found a hardware store with a vast supply of locks. We picked a simple silver one because from a distance it resembled platinum, the hardest, most enduring metal there is. Tradition called for us to engrave our names on the back. But we used a black marker instead. *Laurie and Andrew,* he wrote, in his fanciest script. Then I drew a kind of lop-sided heart around our names, with an arrow going through.

Finding a spot for our lock was the ultimate challenge. By that point there were thousands of locks of every size, shape, and color covering every inch of space on the rails. Many areas were four and five locks deep. All testaments to the enduring power of true love. And ours was one of them.

Now, approaching the bridge on my walk with Richard, I'm filled with dread. I remember exactly where our lock is; it's just past the third lamppost on the right. And I'm trying hard not to remember the moment Andrew kissed me, right after we tossed our key in the water.

Imagine my shock when I see the bridge...and there isn't a lock in sight.

"Wait. Wasn't this once—?"

"Yes," Richard says, anticipating my question. "This is where the love locks used to be."

"What happened?"

"It was too popular. A part of the gate collapsed. Engineers were brought in. They estimated that there were three quarters of a million locks, weighing forty-five tons—the weight of twenty elephants. So they were all cut off."

"And nobody protested?"

"Oh, everybody protested. At one point, the government had to run a love-without-the-locks campaign, asking lovers to set the bridge free. As an ad person, you would have loved it."

"And it worked?"

"Indeed. People went back to declaring their love the old-fashioned way.

"On street corners."

"And what happened to the locks themselves?"

"Sold for scrap, I believe. Local artists were enlisted to create murals to replace them. Let's walk across and you can see a few."

As we get closer, I see the bridge has become a veritable outdoor art gallery. Watercolors, pastels, portraits of nudes, babies, mothers, and assorted Paris landmarks all lean against the sides. There's no trace of what this bridge used to be. It's painful to see.

I am quiet for a moment, lost in thought. I wonder how many of those thousands of lovers are still loving, still together. Richard is watching me. He touches me gently on the shoulder.

"Did you—"

"Yes," I say. "I was married for a while. We spent our honeymoon here.

"At the time, you couldn't be newlyweds without

hearing about the Love Lock Bridge. So yes, one of those locks was—"

I'm about to say *mine*. I correct myself just in time.

"…*Ours*."

He nods. There will be time to tell him about Andrew. But not now. Not here.

He is wise enough to not ask any more questions. He takes my hand with a simple "I'm sorry."

Then we walk across the bridge, back to the hotel.

CHAPTER 20

ONE THING YOU CAN say about Pablo Picasso: he sure understood the madness of love.

My mother and I are spending the afternoon at the Picasso Museum, a glorious seventeenth-century mansion in the Marais district. Lots of misshapen sculptures, off-kilter ceramics, eccentric drawings. But it's the paintings of the women in his life—old, young, fat, skinny, dreamy, distant—that really resonate.

Every early picture of Dora Maar, Olga Khokhlova, and Françoise Gilot starts out the same: in gentle, romantic, pastel hues that capture their deep-seated eyes, a dimple, a shy smile. All are dressed in romantic silks and soft chiffons, their hands pristinely folded on their laps. Beautiful young women, as seen through the eyes of brand-new love.

But keep walking past these, and soon you begin to see cracks.

Same women, slightly different takes. A sharp line here, a raised brow there. The sense of something not quite right. The colors deepen. The portraits become more erotically charged. Dark frowns, outlined in black. Random breasts and penises where they wouldn't ordinarily be.

And then, suddenly, there he is: pure Picasso in full bloom. Paintings of women that are angry, angular, all teeth and genitals. Filled with detached limbs and open mouths that cry out in pain. It's as if every woman, every relationship, was tossed into a Cuisinart, then painted the way they spilled out.

No wonder I left the museum thinking of Andrew.

My mother and I sit at a small outdoor café, sharing another croissant and coffee. A young French couple is sitting at the table near us, gabbing loudly. They are either arguing violently or agreeing violently. The woman has tied her dog, a fluffy white bichon frise, to the table leg. The dog begins to yap. She talks to it in French, waving her hands and shaking her finger at it. The dog quiets down and curls up under the table. I smile. The dog understands French better than I do.

"Did you enjoy the exhibit?" my mother asks.

"I'm not sure 'enjoy' is the word I would use," I say. "It felt like one giant reminder of my marriage."

My mother seems surprised. "How so?" she asks.

"Rosy and wonderful at the beginning. But then, as time wore on . . ."

Yes. *The beginning.* A shipboard romance, literally. I was at my friend Carly's wedding, on one of those party boats that takes you on a slow four-hour sail around Manhattan. As we pulled away from the pier, there was a ceremony. Then a cocktail hour. Then a five-course sit-down dinner, just as the sun was setting over the Hudson River. Carly was an old high school friend. By the time she got engaged, all her other friends were from college or work. I didn't know a soul.

But even without the romantic sunset, Andrew would have been appealing. Tall and slim, with sandy brown hair and brown eyes that looked at you as if his entire life depended on what you were saying. He came up to me at the bar as I was having my second—third? fourth?—glass of wine. He didn't know anybody there, either. He was a distant cousin of the groom.

We talked. We danced. We laughed and talked some more. Andrew was in finance—not a field known for turning out clever, interesting people. But in our first few months together I quickly discovered that Andrew was an anomaly. I rarely understood conversations he had on the phone with his business associates: all about debentures and cash outflow, capped notes and convertible debts. But off the phone he was funny and wise and compassionate. And I fell hard.

"What did you like about Andrew?" I asked my mother. She thinks for a moment.

"He was forthright. He cared about you. Always

looking out for your best interests. And he was never smug the way a lot of successful young men are these days. He seemed . . . kind."

Kind. Yes. I suppose so. When he realized he was still in love with his old flame, he decided he would come clean rather than sneak around behind my back. In fact, he made a big thing out of telling me he wasn't going to sleep with her until after we were legally separated.

"Did you know about the other woman before?" my mother asked.

"I knew he'd been in love. I took that as a hopeful sign. Finally, a man not afraid of commitment. But I didn't know they'd been engaged."

She looks up quickly.

"He was engaged?"

"I never told you the whole story: they'd set the date, then she dumped him for his roommate, married the roommate, then realized she'd made a mistake. By then, Andrew was married to me, but still had feelings for *her*."

"How awful," she says, shaking her head. "How shattered you must have felt."

"Like I was living in a *Dr. Phil* episode," I said. "But I bet you hear all kinds of stories like this in your practice."

"Yes. Men and women who don't know the meaning of monogamous. Men who disappear when they hear the woman is pregnant. Men who stick around and then insist the woman have an abortion, or not have one, claiming it's their right to decide."

"So I guess, next to them, Andrew looks pretty good."

"No," she says gently. "Not if he hurt my girl."

Why do I suddenly feel like I am welling up with tears?

"There's something else I never told you," I say. "I had an abortion when I was younger."

Now it's her turn to be sad.

"Oh, Laurenne," is all she can manage to get out. "You mean he—"

"No," I say. "It wasn't Andrew. It wasn't anybody I cared about. It was—just a fling."

"Not one of the teachers, I hope."

"No," I say, reaching for her uneaten half of the croissant. She doesn't stop me. "Just a guy. His name was Dan. Nice looking, but incredibly boring. And I was suffering from a severe case of sophomore slump. Which made him look all the more appealing."

"Why didn't you tell me?" She wants to know.

"What would you have done?"

She thinks for a moment. I'm hoping she will say *"Comfort you."* But she doesn't.

"I would have put you on to the right people," she says. "A safe place to have it done."

Now I remember why I never told her. I'm not her patient, I'm her daughter.

"I found my own safe place," I say. "It was all fine.

Dan did the right thing—drove me there, split the bill. I didn't see him after that, but it didn't matter. It was no great love match."

"I'm sorry you couldn't tell me before." Then she gestures to the waiter for the check. "Shall we go?"

My mother has a very limited amount of daily sympathy reserves. I think I have exhausted today's supply.

CHAPTER 21

TONIGHT IS DEFINITELY A New Black Dress night.

Richard and I are going to dinner at a fancy bistro. *Fancy* is my word, not his. His word was "ace." I googled the place to check out the dress code. It looks somewhere north of Business Casual and south of Cocktail Party.

There are lots of simple neighborhood bistros scattered all over Paris. Leave it to a true foodie to pick one called Bistrot Kinzo. A Japanese restaurant in the heart of Paris? Well, not quite. According to the website, it's Japanese-French fusion cuisine. Two of his faves, he said. Mine, too.

Kinzo is located on the elegant Right Bank, so Dr. Liz approved. She even complimented me on how good I looked. And I must say, I feel pretty good, too. I checked myself in the full-length mirror before I left.

For the first time in a long time, my hair, makeup, and outfit all seemed to be playing on the same team. I dashed out with a quick wave, and a "Don't wait up!"— words I never had the guts to say when I was a teenager or even in my twenties. Could it be that, in my thirties, I've finally grown a backbone?

I meet Richard in the lobby. I like the way he's looking at my new black dress. His smile tells me he thinks I look hot. But he's too much of a gentleman to say it.

As always, he looks great. A gray suit with an almost invisible black line weave. A charcoal-gray button-down shirt, open at the neck. Side by side we look like something out of *GQ*. And of course, he is wearing great-looking boots. Black, shiny, elaborately single-stitched.

"These are Luccheses," he says, catching my glance. "Their Lonestar Calf Riding Boots. Originally designed for rodeo cowboys and men on horseback."

"Do you ride?" I ask.

"Only in BMWs," he says.

Bistrot Kinzo is in the heart of the 9th arrondissement, near the Palais Garnier, an exquisite beaux arts building that's home to the Paris Opera. The bistro itself is all understated elegance: white marble counters, cherrywood tables and chairs, white sconces gently illuminating everything.

Even the wall decorations are perfectly simple:

graphic prints of brightly colored floating blobs. Salvador Dalí's idea of vegetables.

We are warmly welcomed by the man in front and the chef, both of whom bow ever so slightly—a lovely touch, setting the tone for the evening. Richard and I sit down. Everything here is carefully curated with an eye toward elegance, simplicity, and surprise, starting with a tiny micro towel placed alone in a soup bowl. The waiter lifts a small Japanese teapot and pours boiling water on the towels, which expand to full size.

Richard and I are across from one another, with a great view of the open kitchen.

I look at the menu. Everything sounds exotic and tempting, with ingredients and sauces I don't know.

"I can see why you like this place," I say. "Amazing menu."

He nods. "Unexpected tastes and textures," he says. "Things that surprise the tongue. A sense of adventure on the part of the chef. Fresh, inventive thinking. Probably the same things you look for in creative work."

As different as we are, he is a man who gets me. I like him. I realize this is the first real date I've had, the first man I've cared about, since Andrew and I split three years ago.

"Not to be a wuss," I say, "but perhaps you could order for both of us?"

"I would be thrilled to," he says. "A good meal, like a good friend, should be chosen carefully."

I love that. It sounds so Oscar Wilde.

The waiter comes by for our drink order. I am about to opt for a kiwi martini, but Richard has a better idea.

"Fancy a bottle of champagne?" he says.

"A whole bottle?"

"Do you doubt we can do it justice?"

The champagne arrives, iced in a silver urn. Our waiter pops the cork. It feels like New Year's Eve—new beginnings and the promise of things to come.

"What shall we drink to?" he asks.

"How about: surprises," I say.

"Excellent," he says. We clink glasses. Then he studies the menu. "Tell me about tonight's tasting menu," he says in English to the maître d', who responds in kind.

"Yes, sir. Tonight the soup is pumpkin with enoki mushrooms and chestnut chips. Then a series of smaller plates: Black angus rib steak with sesame. Scallops with leek fondue and wakame seaweed in a yuzu emulsion. Finally tricolor beetroot salad over misozuke salmon."

"Sound good to you?" Richard asks.

"Yes," I say. "I never met a misozuke I didn't like."

The waiter smiles. But Richard laughs.

Plate after elegant plate arrives, a series of beautifully orchestrated dishes of creamy elegant French fused with crunchy savory Japanese. The waiters bow after each course. I feel like I should applaud.

And then, finally, with our café au lait: *le chocolat*. The only way I can describe it is: a mountain of chocolate crème atop a chocolate shell dribbled with chocolate fudge. Not a terrible way to end a meal.

Probably not even a terrible way to end a life.

CHAPTER 22

RECIPE FOR A LOVELY EVENING:

Take one British man with a charming accent. Make sure he has a nice smile and an easy laugh.

Add a warm October night in Paris, one bottle of good French champagne, and some funny anecdotes about your highly unique mother.

Mix well.

Sprinkle in some tales about your wayward former husband. Just a few. Do not over-season.

Add some understanding looks and a nice warm arm around your shoulder as you walk back to the hotel.

Stop under a lamppost.

Kiss, gently. Kiss again.

Laugh when he says, "So who needs locks when you can do this the old-fashioned way?"

Slow down your pace as you walk to the hotel.

Pray to God that your mother is not sitting in the lobby, watching the door. (She isn't.)

Kiss again as you enter the elevator. Hold your breath as you wait to see if he's going to ask you what floor you're on.

Breathe again, when you realize he isn't.

Follow him to his room.

Kiss him before he puts the key in. And then again after.

Notice that all your fears, anxieties, insecurities are . . . melting.

Pour yourself into the chair as he sits on the bed.

Chat a bit more.

In a moment or two, one of you stirs.

Discard the unusable parts (shoes, shirts, black dress).

Carefully slide in next to him on the bed.

Turn up the heat—slowly.

Rock gently.

Blend.

Grind.

Notice how quickly he has brought you to a boil.

Rare. And well done.

Then, about a half hour later: reheat.

And repeat.

CHAPTER 23

THE SUN WAKES ME up. The sun and some clattering around in the bathroom. Richard is up early. I smile, remembering last night. Especially the last few hours before we fell asleep.

I stretch and take a deep breath. I smell aftershave. That means he's already showered. *Too bad.* I was sort of hoping that the two of us could . . .

Then he steps into the room. Fully dressed. Suit, tie, boots, the works.

Even worse: he walks over to the metal suitcase rack. He zips his bag.

"You're up," he says when he sees my eyes are open. There is an awkward — make that deadly — silence.

"I have to leave for London." Then he adds, "But I'll pop back very soon. How could I not?"

More silence.

"It's not what you think," he says. "Something's come up. Please don't look at me like that."

How am I looking at him? I have no idea. My face is frozen. Everything about me is frozen.

"I'll be in touch," he says. He leans over and kisses me. Then he picks up his suitcase and walks out the door, closing it behind him with a gentle click.

I lie in bed, trying to process all this.

Something came up? What? And when, exactly? After we fell asleep? When I went to the ladies' room at the restaurant? Or was it sometime yesterday, but he decided not to tell me till now because he was hoping to . . . No. That's too crass. Or is it? Did he know all along that he'd be saying goodbye this morning? Should I trust him? *Can* I trust him?

In the space of one minute, I go from deliriously happy to totally devastated. I count to thirty slowly, to give him enough time to get into the elevator and down to the lobby. Then I grab my clothes and slip into them, as quickly as I can. I've got to get out of this room. I check the clock. Just past 6 a.m. With any luck, my mother will still be asleep and I can climb into my bed without her knowing.

I look at my phone and see she texted me about a half hour ago. A chill goes through me. It is filled with typos—something my mother would never, ever allow:

Larie please Come bak Need you HeLP

CHAPTER 24

HERE IS A MATH problem for you:

Three people are in an emergency room in a Paris hospital.

One speaks impeccable French (the doctor).

The second also speaks impeccable French but is having trouble getting words out because she's wearing an oxygen mask (the patient).

The third speaks French that can only be described as *peccable* (me).

Question: how long does it take before Person Number Three begins to panic?

The hotel concierge had called for an ambulance. It arrived several hours later. Actually, it was probably only a few minutes later. But in my state of mind, it felt like hours.

As they lifted my mother onto the gurney, she was very quiet. I know she was still in pain and frightened...

because she didn't criticize either me, the EMT workers, or the elevator ride down to the lobby, which also seemed to take hours.

On our way to the hospital, I watch the emergency technicians pull out a series of gadgets and machines designed to measure—*what*? Other than the blood-pressure cuff, I have no idea. I want to ask what's going on. But they don't speak English. Will the doctors?

Just in case, I call Françoise.

She assures me that Georges-Pompidou is *un hôpital excellent* and that she knows several doctors there. Best of all, she promises to head over and join me *immédiatement*.

Our ambulance pulls up outside *les urgences* (the emergency room). The EMT workers slide the gurney down the vehicle's ramp and wheel my mother in. I follow closely behind—still dressed, I might add, in my Walk of Shame wardrobe: a highly wrinkled black dress, uncombed hair, makeup smushed across my face and under my eyes, and high heels. Between my mother and me, we must look like a scene out of some tawdry French movie.

Dr. Boucher, the on-call ER physician, is serious, attentive, and prematurely bald. Since I can't remember the word for "pain," I just grimace and point to my mother's heart (*le cœur*). He nods. Perhaps he doesn't need my help.

I do remember the word for "doctor" (*médecin*) but I can't remember whether it's masculine (*le*) or feminine (*la*). So I just tell him, *"Elle est médecin,"* which simply translates as "she is doctor." I want him to understand why my mother may be a somewhat difficult patient.

Soon they wheel over an EKG machine. My mother is hooked up to a set of electrodes on her chest, arms, and legs. Seconds later, a piece of graph paper slides out of the machine, filled with hills and valleys that indicate the state of her heart. The doctor looks at it and nods again. I can't read his expression. He shows the paper to my mother. She reads it and tries to speak, but the oxygen mask is getting in her way. She lifts it up to make a point. That's when Dr. Boucher gets annoyed.

Another scene in the bad French movie: my mother and the doctor arguing; he is trying to hold the mask on her face and she is trying to wrench it off to speak.

Just then Françoise arrives. I am tempted to hug her. But there's no time for that. She waves to my mother and introduces herself to Dr. Boucher, who, in a great flurry of fast French, quickly updates her about possible next steps. I hear a lot of letters thrown around that sound like advanced college degrees: EKGs, CCTAs, MRIs.

Françoise tries to do a quick simultaneous translation. But somewhere along the way she decides to just sum it up.

I suppose that's better. But as I'm waiting, I keep

imagining Worst Possible Scenarios. What if it's serious? What if my mother needs emergency heart surgery? Do we stay in Paris? For how long? Should I look into getting us an apartment instead of our pricey hotel?

And even worse than the Worst Case: suppose my mother never makes it out of Paris? What if she dies? How do I get her body home? Do I have it cremated first? How does my mother even feel about cremation?

And why have I never discussed any of this with her before?

What I thought was a simple panic attack on my part is quickly morphing into full-blown terror. I feel myself getting light-headed. *Are these chest pains I'm feeling?* No. Probably just anxiety. When Françoise turns to tell me what's going on, I wave her off. I sit down and take a few deep breaths.

The good news: if I start to pass out, I'm in the right place.

After a lot of back-and-forth conversation, Dr. Boucher, Dr. Liz, and Françoise have come to a unified point of view. As Françoise tells me: it's probably not a true cardiac arrest, which could have been deadly, but something more minor. (Can *minor* really be the word for anything connected with the heart?) Something that can be controlled with medication or a minor (there's that word again) procedure. They'd like to admit her for a day and give her some tests to make sure, especially given her recent heart trouble back in America. Meanwhile, Françoise will stay in close touch.

A nurse closes the curtain around the ER bed to let my mother get some sleep while they try to locate a room. Meanwhile, Françoise puts a reassuring hand on my shoulder.

"Laurie, I'm so glad you called," she says.

"Not as glad as I am," I say. She smiles. To her credit, she doesn't mention anything about how I look or how I am dressed. Maybe Walk-of-Shame-wear is not an uncommon sight here in the City of Love.

CHAPTER 25

ONCE MY MOTHER IS asleep, Françoise and I wander over to the family lounge. It's the first moment I've had to look around. As hospitals go, this one is quite beautiful. Like a modern luxury hotel. Sleek and elegant on the outside—all glass and steel with a bold architectural design of unexpected angles. Inside, various corridors are separated with glass panes that let the light shine through. There's even an indoor glass-covered walkway dotted with palm trees.

"I've brought all my classwork here with me," Françoise says, pulling out her iPad. "So if you want to go back to the hotel and get some rest, I'll stay with her. If anything comes up, I can handle it. And I'll call you."

I *would* like to shower, change, dress, maybe even take a nap. But I'm torn. Will my mother feel like I deserted her again?

"I appreciate your concern," I tell Françoise. "Really, I do. But..."

Françoise is going to make a wonderful doctor. She knows exactly why I'm hesitating.

"Listen to me," she says. "When your mother wakes up, who would she rather discuss her medical issues with? A daughter? Or a doctor?"

"I get your drift," I say, tucking my guilt back inside where it belongs.

Now that the pressure is off for a while, I take a look around. It is less hectic here than at most emergency rooms I've been in. True, it's early morning. Still, no one is "bleeding out" or moaning; no loved ones are standing around sobbing or yelling at the doctors. Unlike American hospitals, this one is not painted ugly pea-soup green. It is white, clean, pristine, and highly efficient. Even the ER patients seem relaxed.

Françoise assures me that my mother is in good hands here: this is the hospital where a team of doctors implanted the very first artificial heart made of bio-materials and electronic sensors.

I'm glad I left Richard Northcott's room as quickly as I did. I'm glad Françoise is here for moral and medical support.

Most of all, I'm glad it will take a few days before I learn that the doctor's name—Boucher—is the French word for *butcher*.

CHAPTER 26

AT THE HOTEL I shower, wash my hair, take a short nap, then quickly return to the hospital. When I enter my mother's room, I see Françoise has pulled a chair up to her bed and is sitting there holding her hand.

My mother is awake and frowning.

Françoise gets up and hugs me. "She's good," she says as if my mother is not in the room. "So far, all indications are that it's atrial fibrillation. A-fib, as we call it."

And that means...?

"An irregular heartbeat. In this case it's probably paroxysmal atrial fibrillation."

And that means...?

"It means that her symptoms come and go. They can last from a few minutes to several hours. Sometimes even a week or more. Most times they go away by themselves."

I try to think back to what Dr. Akers said in New Jersey about my mother's condition, and how this new diagnosis compares. But I'm too anxious to remember most of the specifics. Even if I could, I'm not sure I'd know what questions to ask.

What I do ask is, "And if her symptoms *don't* go away on their own?"

"If they're persistent she may need some additional treatment," Françoise says. "Medication can control it. Or sometimes an electric shock can do the trick."

She sees me blanch.

"Don't worry," she says, laughing. "If you're thinking of all those horror movies where they tie you down and shave your head before they put giant iron clamps on—it's not like that. It's a simple procedure called cardioversion. You're asleep through it. You don't even remember it when you're up."

So why is my mother frowning?

"They want me to wear a *monitor,*" she says.

A monitor?

"A Holter monitor," Françoise says. "Strapped to her chest. It's only for twenty-four hours. It will measure her heart rhythms over a twenty-four-hour period. However," she says, smiling at my mother, "I'm sensing some pushback."

Pushback, from Dr. Liz? Imagine that.

"I will not be able to take a shower for twenty-four hours," my mother says, making a face. "And since I didn't get to take one this morning, that will make it forty-eight hours."

But that's not the worst of it.

"It will look ludicrous under my clothes."

You know what they say about how doctors make the worst patients? Well, consider it true.

"Mother," I say in the gentlest tone I can. "What if you were advising a patient, and the patient reacted the way you are?"

"You forget," she says. "Patients are people. But I...am...*invincible.*"

There is a brief moment when I worry that she may have become truly delusional. But then she starts to laugh. Frankly, it could have gone either way.

So Dr. Liz agrees to stay in the hospital overnight for tests, and wear a Holter monitor for one day when she gets out.

We sit there for a while, waiting to see when her tests will be scheduled. At one point I excuse myself. Per the hospital's rules, I have turned my phone off. I head back to the family lounge and turn it on again to see if Richard has left a message.

He hasn't. But my office has.

I haven't had a chance to read the meeting reports Drew emailed me but I call him back anyway. He updates me on the latest info on the health and beauty market. The magic words these days are *texture, exfoliating scalp care,* and *plant inclusions.* Then he fills me in on some nice juicy pieces of office gossip. Allison refuses to work with Sarah. Lance is not happy with his raise. And yes, just as everybody suspected: Madelyn told everyone that she's sleeping with Ryan.

It is now late afternoon. I head back up to my mother's room.

"You two can go," my mother says, looking at the clock. "They may not be taking me around for tests for a few hours. Go have something to eat. I'll be fine."

I look at Françoise. "Is this a good idea?"

"Yes," she says. "Any results they get from tonight's tests, your mother asked her doctors to call or text me."

"You two deserve a nice dinner together, on me," my mother says, in a sweeping move of generosity. I guess she's forgotten my overnight sojourn with the man she does not approve of.

Françoise and I head out for a quiet relaxing dinner together.

Except it doesn't turn out that way.

CHAPTER 27

I'M FREEZING. AND I'M loving every minute of it.

We are sitting and shivering in an improbable place called Le Kube—an ice bar made entirely of twenty tons of ice, with igloo ice-block counters and frozen ice-cube walls.

When we first arrived, they took our jackets and gave us two of theirs—one green, one yellow, both down-filled and thermal-lined, with matching gloves. The bar area is illuminated with bright neon lights that glow pink and purple and royal blue. Several faux-fur blankets are scattered around so you can wrap yourself in them. I see several couples cuddling for extra warmth.

"What do you think of this place?" Françoise asks.

"Totally surreal," I say. It's not an exaggeration. Le Kube is visually stunning. Just this side of a post-apocalyptic world where time has stopped.

I said it was freezing, but did I mention exactly *how* freezing? A whopping -18 degrees Celsius. For us Fahrenheit-loving Americans, that would be equal to -4. It's so cold, in fact, that they limit your time here to twenty-five minutes.

I look around. Customers are posing on giant ice cubes while they take selfies. They joke about how cold their bottoms are. The Americans are talking about their butts. The French are laughing about their *derrières,* which sounds so much classier.

"This place is definitely cool, especially after the day I've had," I tell Françoise. "The perfect spot to chill out."

She laughs. "See? That's why we're here," she says. "I was afraid if I brought a creative person like you to an ordinary French bar you'd be bored."

I'm not sure I would've been bored at a regular bar, but she's right. I am loving the quirkiness of this place. It will be a great story when I get back home.

Françoise suggests we order the house specialty: vodka in a frosty chilled glass. Sounds good.

The vodka warms me but also makes me a little woozy. It occurs to me that I haven't eaten all day. Almost unheard of, for me. I guess I had too much on my mind to think about food—till now.

"I'm hungry," I say.

Right next door to Le Kube is a typical French

restaurant with crisp white tablecloths and the *spécial-ités de la maison* written with brightly colored markers on chalkboards. We pick a table near the window so I can look out and watch the world (*le monde*) go by. The restaurant is small and cozy, but it still takes me a while to get warm again.

The waiter comes by with a menu. I'm all over it. *Soupe à l'oignon* seems especially inviting: piping hot, with melted cheese. I order that and coq au vin, plus a bottle of Perrier.

Françoise says she's not hungry. She doesn't even take a piece of bread.

"A double Grey Goose straight up," she says.

Our waiter comes back with our drinks and pours the Perrier into my glass. It's cold, but not icy. Françoise and I clink glasses. Tonight's toast is an obvious one: to my mother's health.

I take a few sips. Françoise, meanwhile, has downed quite a bit of her vodka. The effects are starting to show. Her perfect English seems a little less perfect. She thinks hard about every word she's about to say. But, hey, she's had a tense day, too. She's unwinding.

She slugs the rest of the vodka, and gestures to the waiter for a refill.

She is still beautiful, but I'm beginning to see cracks in the veneer. As she downs vodkas number three and number four, it's making me a bit anxious. The woman

I'm counting on for major medical advice—the liaison between my mother and the entire Parisian medical system—is slurring her words.

Another sip, and Françoise struggles to speak. "Laurie, I'm not... you seem to... why are you so...?" She can't seem to get her thoughts together.

"I like you," she says at last. "And I like your... your..."

She lets the sentence hang in midair as she searches for the right word. Finally, she finds it. "Your *mother*. Nice, nicer than mine."

Then she goes off on a tirade: how cold her mother is, unfeeling, never loved her enough, is disappointed in her canceling the wedding, on and on and on.

She orders another vodka. Now what? This almost-perfect person seems to be losing control. Suddenly I am the one in charge. I need to finish my dinner so I can help her get home.

As I take my last bite, Françoise excuses herself and goes to the ladies' room. She's there a very long time. I pay the check, then go to look for her.

When I swing the door open, I'm shocked at what I see: Françoise is sitting on the tile floor with her head cocked to one side, singing a nursery rhyme in French.

Alouette, gentille alouette,
Alouette, je te plumerai.
Je te plumerai le bec...

"C'mon, Françoise," I say, "let's get you home." *But where exactly is home?*

I ask her. She shrugs.

I search her purse and get lucky. I find a small paper card tucked into a pocket that reads: *"Veuillez retournez à 11, rue Jacob."*

Outside, I hail a cab and somehow manage to get her in it. She keeps saying she doesn't feel well. She looks like hell.

When we pull up to her address, I search her bag for keys and finally figure out which is for the downstairs door and which is for the apartment.

Of course, just to add to the adventure: it's a walk-up. Somehow we stumble up the three flights. I lean her against the wall as I open her door.

Even with the lights off, I can tell it's a lovely place. A marble fireplace. A small loveseat in dark velvet. I lead her into the bedroom and plop her down on the bed. She murmurs a few things I don't understand. I'm not even sure if she's speaking English or French. At one point I hear her mumble something about someone named "Ben Shore." Or maybe it was *"bien sûr."*

I would love to get a look at her place, but now is not the time. I just want to get out of there. I leave her keys on a table, turn out the lights, and run downstairs to get another taxi.

I think of how jealous I was of her, the first day we met. She seemed so perfect. But it's clear she's got her own problems. I don't take any pleasure in that. She's a lovely person. I feel sorry for her.

I hail another cab and head back to the hotel. I check: no texts, messages, or phone calls from my mother or the hospital.

And nothing from Richard Northcott, either.

CHAPTER 28

THE HOLTER MONITOR IS a huge inconvenience for Dr. Liz. And Dr. Liz does not like to be inconvenienced.

It's a small but somewhat clunky thing she wears on a strap around her neck. She doesn't like the way it "stands out" under her shirt. She's even less happy with how it looks under her sweaters: like a third—square—breast.

"Why don't you wear it on the outside, like a quirky piece of jewelry?" I ask. She glares at me. I forgot: she's invincible. It would be as if Superman showed up with his arm in a sling.

The good news is, she's up, walking around and complaining about the hospital. Too much wait time between tests. The staff was "snippy." (Dr. Liz–speak for *They didn't wait on me hand and foot.*)

"And considering this is France," she says, "the food was inedible."

Dr. Boucher advises my mother not to stay in bed. The monitor is designed to register what a typical day is like, so he urges her to go out and walk around. It's another beautiful Parisian day. We decide to go to lunch, and rather than choose a restaurant in advance, we'll play it by ear.

Dr. Liz is still grumbling about the "encumbrance" around her neck as we stroll around the Île de la Cité, checking out various window menus.

Suddenly there is a loud screech. A blue Citroën has stopped short in front of a man who was crossing the street haphazardly. The driver gets out and starts yelling at the man. But something is not right. The man turns to the driver and says nothing. Then, slowly, he begins collapsing to the pavement.

The driver looks confused, then shocked. Was this his fault? Did he hit the man without realizing it?

Cars backed up behind the driver begin to blare their horns. People rush toward the man lying in the street. He opens his mouth and tries to speak, but nothing comes out.

My mother pushes her way through the crowd. Alarmed, I follow suit.

She bends down next to the man and takes his pulse. She loosens his tie and pulls his shirt out of his slacks. She shakes him. No response. She screams at him: *"Monsieur! Monsieur!"* Still no response. A woman reaches for her phone and calls for an ambulance, which in French sounds like *oon am-bu-lonz*.

By this point, the man is unconscious. My mother begins chest compressions, pushing down with both hands. He's gasping. She quickens the pace—harder, faster. He seems to have stopped breathing. One push every second, then letting his chest rise again after each push. A few seconds of this, and she begins calling out a series of letters: "AED! AED!"

A worker from a nearby restaurant rushes out and hands my mother a small machine with two adhesive strips. She rips open the man's shirt and puts one strip on the top left over his heart, the second on the bottom right. She pushes a button. The man's body jumps, then jumps again. She keeps pushing. Finally, his eyes open. There's a breath, the very beginning of a smile.

By now the ambulance has arrived. Two workers jump out and put the man on a stretcher. As my mother takes a step back, the crowd begins to applaud her.

"Vous êtes un héros, madame!" they yell out. *"Non!"* somebody shouts. *"Une héroïne!"*

My mother smiles, looks around, and bows. "Merci," she says. Somebody snaps her picture.

Dr. Liz seems none the worse for wear. While *I* am sweating profusely, worrying about her stamina. Just then, an older man who seems like the owner of the restaurant comes out and shakes my mother's hand.

"Entrez, mesdames, pour votre repas de fête. Gratu-itement."

"Pas necessaire," says my mother. But the man will not take *non* for an answer.

"J'insiste," he says, taking her arm, leading her into the restaurant for a free celebratory lunch. I follow behind.

Inside, he hits a spoon on a glass to get everyone's attention. Then he makes a big announcement, beginning with "Voici la femme qui..."

This is the woman who...

All the patrons stand up and applaud her. My mother is beaming.

Under her shirt, that Holter monitor must be lighting up like a pinball machine.

CHAPTER 29

ACCORDING TO THE HOLTER monitor results, my mother's heart is fine. Perhaps a little too fine.

Hours later, after a big celebratory lunch, we are having a glass of Sancerre near the Champs-Élysées with Emil Beux, an old University of Wisconsin–Madison professor of mine. Dr. Beux and I have kept in touch ever since French 101.

I hated him at first: tall, ridiculously skinny, and unnecessarily sarcastic, with a thin, villainous-looking mustache. The first day of class, Monsieur Beux wrote his name on the blackboard and went around the classroom asking us to pronounce it. One by one, we guessed.

"Byoox?"

"Bux?"

"Boox?"

"Bee-ux?"

He smirked and shook his head no.

"It's pronounced *Buh*," he said, correcting us. And then (sarcastically) added: "It rhymes with *Duh*."

But by the end of the semester, I grew to like him a lot more. When I visited Paris my junior year, I knew he had moved back, so I reached out and made it a point to meet him for a drink. I did so again with Andrew during our honeymoon. Today, Monsieur Beux has grown into a distinguished older man. Gray hair the color of steel wool, crow's feet and wrinkles that tell of a life well lived. And either the same perfect white teeth he's always had, or the world's best dentures.

But never in my wildest dreams did I ever consider him a heartthrob.

And yet—and I don't think one glass of wine is enough to distort my perceptions—I could swear my mother is flirting with him.

She is wearing a fire-engine red pantsuit and black patent leather heels. As always, she has taken great pains getting dressed. And it shows: she looks great.

Dr. Beux has chosen the perfect place to meet— Le Rooftop, the bar on top of the Peninsula Paris hotel, with a spectacular view of the sunset. As always, he looks like the ideal college professor, down to the brown suede elbow patches on his tweed jacket. He kisses me on both cheeks.

"This is my mother, Dr. Liz Ormson," I say. "She speaks French better than I do."

"This is indeed a pleasure," he says. Then he kisses her the same way.

Dr. Liz is immediately smitten.

"Tell me how you've been," he says as we take our seats. I rattle off everything we've seen and done since we arrived. I wait for my mother to add her saga of the *Hôpital Georges-Pompidou*. Interestingly, she doesn't.

"And you?" I ask. "Still teaching?"

"Yes," he says, "French as a second language for foreign students—mostly adult immigrants. Quite refreshing, having students who really *want* to learn."

He winks at my mother. She giggles. Not laughs. *Giggles!*

Could this be the way she always acts around men? I don't know. I haven't seen her around any since my dad died six years ago.

"And how's your family?" I ask.

Mr. Beux was married when he was my teacher, with two children a little younger than me. Since then, he explains, a lot of life has happened. "My daughter, Genevieve, is married with a baby of her own on the way."

"How nice for you," my mother says.

"And André is getting a master's in history. I guess he'll follow in my footsteps as a teacher at some point," he says.

Then his voice gets quiet. He swallows. "But a year ago, after a long illness, my Marianne died."

"I'm so sorry," my mother and I both say.

He does a fast update: the sudden pain, the quick diagnosis, the months she lingered. How he and the children huddled by her bedside the last few days. I remember his classroom persona: quick, brusque, just this side of snide. Now he takes his time speaking. He weighs his words carefully, as if they are in limited supply.

My mother is listening very hard. She looks at him and speaks gently.

"There's no good way to die," she says. "Fast, slow. It's all heartbreaking. I'm a widow myself."

A wave of relief rolls across his face, so thick it's almost palpable. You can see what he's thinking: *Someone who understands. A kindred spirit.*

She tells him about my father and how he lingered. And with that, they begin a serious discussion about love, loss, the stages of grief, and moving on. This is the kindly, sympathetic side of Dr. Ormson that her patients know. The side I rarely see. I sit and listen as the two of them comfort one another.

I gaze around. The sun is going down. Halfway through my second glass of wine, I realize they are both speaking French. I don't remember when this started. I catch a word or two, but not much. Now they're giggling together. He points out something on the menu that he thinks she might like. Something in a cream sauce.

"Not for me," she says in English. "But Laurie might enjoy that."

He looks up. He seems surprised to still see me there.

I order *bœuf bourguignon* and mashed potatoes. I'm trying to figure out the difference between their ages. She's sixty-eight. He's got to be at least ten years younger. *How ironic*. I'd been worried my mother would feel like the third wheel as he and I chatted on and on about old college memories. Turns out, *I'm* the extra wheel here tonight. I'm trying desperately not to be squeaky.

Dinner comes. I push the meat around on my plate and dive into the comforting mashed potatoes. Dessert is homemade *glace,* vanilla and chocolate, ice cold and soothing.

"This was a treat," Mr. Beux says, as the check comes. "Two lovely ladies for the price of one." He takes out his wallet. But I insist on paying. He protests. Finally, he relents.

"Since it's still early . . . how would you feel about a walk?" he asks.

"Not for me," I say. Few things make me feel as left out as a three-person walk. Even under ordinary circumstances, I'm usually the one walking behind the other two. "I need to get back and catch up on some office work."

"Then I guess we two will have to make do on our own," Mr. Beux says to my mother. Then he winks at her.

Now wait a minute...
Is he flirting?
Are they going to...?
Would he ever even suggest...?

I've been tongue-tied in the past. But this is something new. It's like I'm *brain-tied*. I see how they've been looking at each other. I can't even put a simple sentence together.

CHAPTER 30

I HAVE NO IDEA what time my mother gets back.

I tried like crazy to stay awake. I wasn't worried. But it would have been amusing to see what the perfectly put-together Dr. Liz looked like on her very own Walk of Shame—if, indeed, there was any shame to walk away from.

But I blew it. I fell asleep.

By the time I wake up, she is fully dressed and entirely unforthcoming.

"Good morning," she says.

"Good morning," I say. I lie there for a few moments, chuckling to myself, trying to figure out how to handle the elephant in the room. I'd like to ask where she was. No. Actually, I'm dying to come right out with it: *"Did you two do it? C'mon, girl. Spill!"* But I doubt this will go over well.

Instead, I ask, "How did you sleep?"

"Fine," she replies.

Daughter grilling mother. Our roles have suddenly reversed. I look her up and down, trying to sense even the slightest change in her demeanor, a hint of what might have happened last night.

She's inscrutable. She doesn't blink, doesn't blush. I try another tack.

"Mr. Beux really seemed to enjoy talking to you," I say, carefully opening the door to a real conversation.

"Yes," she says. Door closed.

Today's the day we're headed to Sacré-Cœur in Montmartre, arguably the most magnificent view in all of Paris. I jump in the shower. As I towel myself off, I think of another opening line. *Worth a try.*

"You okay to walk around today?" I ask as I dry my hair.

"Yes. Why wouldn't I be?"

"You were gone for a long time last night. And those heels you were wearing..."

"I'm fine," she says. Another short staccato answer.

At some point, I will have to get her drunk to learn the truth.

CHAPTER 31

MONTMARTRE IS THE HIGHEST point in all of Paris. And Abbesses, the nearest station, is the deepest Métro stop in the city. Even after we take an elevator, we still have several flights of stairs to climb. It's endless. As is the long, white-tiled tunnel to the street.

Montmartre is known as an artists' haven. Van Gogh and Picasso spent a lot of time here. Other artists soon followed. We stroll through the Place du Tertre, a vibrant open-air art gallery packed with colorful artist stalls and equally colorful artists. All of them are willing to draw our portraits for a small fee. *Non, merci.* We keep walking.

Right across from Sacré-Cœur is Saint-Pierre de Montmartre, one of the oldest surviving churches in the city. A crowd is gathered on the steps. Soon the massive iron church doors swing open, and a bride and groom walk out holding hands. They look like models for the top of a wedding cake. The crowd begins throwing rice at them. The couple ducks down, laughing, and the groom puts his arm around his new wife. It's a beautiful, joyful sight. And it makes me sad.

"Did I look that happy as a bride?" I ask my mother.

"Of course," she replies. But what she says next takes me totally by surprise. "When did things start to get bad between you and Andrew?"

Funny. My mother knows a lot about the wedding, and thanks to this trip, a lot more now about the divorce. But the marriage? That's something we've never talked about. *Where to begin?*

"Well, it wasn't like what you and Dad had," I say. "Your marriage was so..."

"Long?" she asks.

"I was going to say *perfect*."

She shakes her head. "'Perfect' only happens in fairy tales."

"Okay, then. You seemed so perfect *together*. I'm not sure Andrew and I ever felt like that."

We watch as the new bride and groom hug their guests. Some of them are crying.

"Dad was always so devoted to you," I say.

"Yes," my mother agrees. For a moment she is lost in thought.

"I never really got that sense from Andrew. He wasn't like Dad."

"My dear, most men are not."

The newlyweds get into a white stretch limousine. The car pulls away as the crowd watches and waves. Slowly, the wedding guests begin to scatter.

"Your father was a very special man," she says. "Really old-world, in a way a lot of men aren't. He believed in chivalry, in taking care of a woman."

"And you liked that?"

"God, no!" she says. "I felt smothered! Couldn't bear it. Me, dependent on someone else? *Me?*"

We have reached the bottom of the hill. The great basilica looms above us, and now we have a choice. We can hike the 270 steps leading up to the top. Or we can ride the funicular.

"Your father used to say I had a hard shell," she says. "Do you think so?"

Yes, I want to say. *Absolutely. Tough as nails. Inflexible.* But she seems so trusting at this moment, I don't have the heart.

"You do have kind of a shell," I say carefully. "But it's like the candy coating on an M&M."

We join the group of people waiting to board the funicular, which is pulling into view. The line is short. It moves quickly. There's plenty of room for us.

"Still, I know I made your father happy. He always told me I was the great love of his life."

"Was he the great love of yours?" I ask.

My mother doesn't answer. Which takes me by surprise.

The funicular starts grinding its way to the top. We hear lots of mechanical squeaks and squeals.

"Was he?" I ask again.

Still no answer. All around, people are taking selfies and videos as the city of Paris slowly reveals itself beneath us. As we get closer to the top, I hear the strains of "Amazing Grace"and see a man seated right outside the basilica, singing as he strums a small, battered harp.

"There was somebody else," my mother says at long last.

"The young man at the kiosk? Yes, you told me."

"Not him," she says. "Somebody far more important." My mother takes a deep, whistling breath. She tilts her head as she looks at me. "It didn't work out."

At that exact moment, the funicular stops in its tracks. So do I.

The view, as every guidebook promises, is stunning. But no more stunning than what my mother has just revealed. *She married my father on the rebound?*

Exactly the way Andrew married me.

CHAPTER 32

IT SOUNDED PERFECT.

A VIP private full-day tour of Versailles Palace, Grand Trianon, Petit Trianon, Marie Antoinette's private rural hamlet, and the royal gardens in a Wi-Fi-equipped Mercedes-Benz with your own personal guide.

And it would have been...if we hadn't missed the limo.

So instead of relaxing in a luxury limo, my mother and I stand on a street corner, acting out our latest installment of the Liz 'n' Laurie Blame Game.

HER: I *told* you we should have left earlier! If you hadn't dawdled...

ME: Dawdled? How? By taking a shower? By getting dressed? *You're* the one who said an hour should be plenty of time to get to—

HER: No! I said an hour *and a half*. But *you* said that was too much.

ME: And I also said *let's take the Métro*. But *you* insisted on a cab. *You* should have made the arrangements!

HER: You're right. *I* would have insisted they pick us up at the hotel.

So here we are, two harridans screaming at each other on a street corner in the City of Love. People walking by shake their heads. Two very ugly—and very loud—Americans.

But one little lady walking by stops and listens to us for a while. She's tiny, barely five feet tall, and about the same age as my mother. Although she's dressed in ordinary street clothes, as she comes closer, I see she's wearing a nun's white wimple around her head.

"Excuse me," the nun says in English. My mother and I stop in mid-blame and look up. "I couldn't help overhearing you."

How embarrassing. We have become a public nuisance.

"It's so hard to judge the traffic these days," she says in a lovely French accent. "I am Sister Delphine. And I am so sorry you missed your ride to Versailles."

"That's very sweet of you," my mother says, suddenly appalled at having aired our dirty laundry in public.

"But you do not need Versailles. There's something just as beautiful right near here," Sister Delphine says.

My mother and I look at each other. We're both thinking the same thing: *yet another stained-glass church.*

"That's very kind," my mother says. "But we've already seen so many of your lovely churches."

The nun laughs. "Oh, it's not a church. And it's not a museum. But I promise you, it is magnificent. Most people never even get to see the inside."

Hmmm. Not a church. Not a museum. And something that even a nun would enjoy? Such a delicious potpourri of clues. Intrigued, my mother and I decide it's worth a look. We turn and follow her.

On the way, we learn that Sister Delphine is a Carmelite nun. She entered the order at nineteen, spent many years teaching in Africa and Mexico, and has just recently come back to her old convent in Neuilly.

We turn a corner.

"There it is," declares Sister Delphine. "The Palais Garnier. The French Opera House."

"You must be an opera fan," I say as we walk toward the exquisite building. Two gilded copper statues flank an entrance that's covered with busts of the Muses and gorgeous ornamentation.

Sister Delphine smiles shyly. "Actually...I am an opera *singer*."

We must look shocked. She laughs.

"I know," she says. "The Singing Nun. I've heard all the jokes! But I was an opera singer long before I was called to serve God. I come from a simple family," Sister Delphine continues. "But my parents had a lot of opera records. I used to sing along with them when I was just a girl."

"Did you take lessons?" I ask.

She nods. "I was told I had the makings of a fine soprano. But after school, I was like a lot of young girls. I was confused. I had *two* callings. I had to make a choice."

We step inside the opera house and look around. It's like walking into a gold-encrusted Baroque sandcastle. The opulence is stunning—and humbling. After our ugly street scene, my mother and I are both at a loss for words.

"You need not buy a performance ticket," Sister Delphine says. "You can sign up for a tour, right here."

We do. The next tour starts in ten minutes. Dr. Liz and I wait at the foot of a breathtaking green and white Italian marble Grand Staircase, underneath a massive brass and crystal chandelier the size of a New York City studio apartment. Carved gold-leaf cherubim and nymphs cover the ceiling. There are mosaics everywhere, and a center fresco by Chagall. It's hard to believe Versailles—or any place in the world—could be more magnificent than this.

"And check this out," I say to my mother, pointing at something in the tour pamphlet. "On the second floor there's a hall of mirrors."

Sister Delphine nods. "Yes. Napoleon insisted his architect design one like the original in Versailles. Many think Garnier's is even more beautiful. And if you've ever heard of *The Phantom of the Opera*..."

"Of course," I say. *Who hasn't?* The famous Gothic romance novel—and Andrew Lloyd Webber musical—about a disfigured musical genius who seduced a poor young soprano right here, in the underground cellar.

"Then make sure you see the plaque outside Loge 5, the Loge du Fantôme de l'Opéra. The Phantom's balcony hideout. It's always empty, ready for the ghost of the Phantom, should it ever return."

"You mean it's been here *before*...?"

"So they say."

We say *au revoir* to Sister Delphine. But I still have one question.

"You had two callings," I say. "And you loved them both. How did you decide which one to follow?"

She smiles. It is obviously a question she has been asked before.

"It happened right here, in 1976," she says. "I was in the balcony as the great soprano Margaret Price sang a magnificent rendition of 'Dove Sono.' I realized that although I was a good singer, I would never be as good as her. So I decided to put that dream aside. I knew what my true path should be."

"You were lucky," says my mother. "Most people go through life never knowing."

"Of course, I did have a little help deciding," she adds mysteriously.

"Pressure from your family?" I ask, thinking of all the times my mother tried to persuade me to go to law school.

"No," Sister Delphine says, smiling. I swear I see a twinkle in her eye as she says, "The opera I heard that day? It was Poulenc's *Dialogues of the Carmelites.*"

She hugs us both. And she is gone.

CHAPTER 33

WHAT KIND OF DAUGHTER brings her recently hospitalized mother to visit a cemetery?

It sounds like the beginning of a riddle. And in any other city, it might be. But Paris is home to *Père Lachaise*—a cemetery that's become a huge tourist attraction. Certainly because of its serene beauty, but mostly because of the famous people buried there.

The cemetery opened in 1804. At first, nobody was interested. *Too far from the city for a funeral,* they said. Definitely too far for weekly visits from grieving families.

Then Napoleon had a great idea: dig up a few famous bodies from other cemeteries—the playwright Molière, the fabulist La Fontaine—and rebury them here. *Bingo.* Lachaise became *the* go-to place for both the living and the dead.

When my mother and I arrive at the gate, we buy a

guidebook. Almost a million people are buried here; a million headstones, mausoleums, and tombs. Most are regular, little-known Parisians. But it's also the resting place for some great artists: actress Sarah Bernhardt, composer Frédéric Chopin, dancer Isadora Duncan, and authors Gertrude Stein, Marcel Proust, and Honoré de Balzac, among many others.

As we walk around, we discover that certain graves have become magnets for groupies. Poet and playwright Oscar Wilde's tomb, which has a sphinxlike naked flying angel, is surrounded by Plexiglas covered with scribbled messages and lipstick kisses. The grave of musician Jim Morrison is cordoned off by metal barricades, though that doesn't stop adoring fans from leaving behind the detritus of a rock 'n' roll life well lived: candles, flowers, empty bottles of wine, even drug paraphernalia.

"This does not look like any cemetery I've ever seen," my mother comments. She's right. Five thousand tall, scattered trees—oak, maple, ash, and chestnut—make it look more like an elegant park. There is nothing sad about this place.

"It's so soothing here, so quiet and peaceful," I say. "I bet that's the big draw of this place. It makes death seem that way, too." She nods.

Still, as we walk, I can tell that something is beginning to weigh Dr. Liz down. My mother seems a little...distracted? With her recent heart issues, this may not have been the wisest place to bring her. Even though it was her idea.

I decide to lighten the moment with a dopey joke I remember from junior high school.

ME: I bet you don't know what makes this place so popular.

HER: What?

ME: People are dying to get in.

She smiles, a half smile.

"Are you thinking about Dad?"

"Yes," she says, "as well as my parents and Grandma Miriam, and all the friends I've lost over the years."

As a doctor, my mother is no stranger to death. I know she cut open a formaldehyde-filled body or two in medical school, and probably barely blinked. She looked so stoic at my father's funeral. But maybe on the inside she was hurting more than I realized.

"You never get used to death," she says. "We are all here for such a brief time and then it's over . . . but never for the ones left behind." She's beginning to sound like a Hallmark card. That worries me. *Where's that tough outer shell when we need it?*

I see a small crowd ahead, mostly young women and a few couples, giggling and taping notes to a headstone. As we get closer, we see it's the double-width grave of Abélard and Héloïse, the scandalous medieval lovers now buried together in a single coffin.

My mother reads from the guidebook: "Over the

years, many lovers leave notes here—either celebrating their own love or seeking advice. And singles and the lovelorn leave desperate letters of hope."

"I hope I'm never that desperate," I say. For a split second I think about Richard Northcott. *Two ships that passed in the night.* I look at my mother, still lost in thought.

"Do you ever think about dying?" I ask.

"No more than most people my age," she says.

"Do you think there's anything after this?"

"You mean, does the spirit survive? Will we meet up with our loved ones in the Great Hereafter? How nice it would be to see your father again. Or Doris."

Doris, my mother's best friend, died several years ago. She had a constant cough that wouldn't go away. It turned out to be an early sign of esophageal cancer. But not early enough.

"But no, I don't believe it," she says.

My mother is a scientist at heart and a big believer in the scientific method. An experiment has to be replicable over and over with different scientists under the same conditions with the same results for her to believe them.

"What about all the people declared dead, then coming back to life?" I say. "All those stories about long tunnels, bright white lights..."

"Just *stories*," she says.

"So you don't worry about dying?"

"I worry it might be painful...for you," my mother says. "I don't want you to suffer because of me."

I am so touched by this that I'm tempted to hug her. But that would startle both of us. Instead, I settle for a simple arm around her shoulders.

Plato once said that all learning is really relearning. My recurring lesson is to keep reminding myself that what feels like nagging is just her worrying about me. My mother worries that I'm eating too much or too little. She worries that I don't know how to dress myself, or choose a man, or keep a man, or pay my rent.

"I know you'll be okay on your own," she says, "but still..."

And then, because I don't know what else to add, I say "Thank you."

Deep down, it's nice to know that tough, overbearing Dr. Liz is in my corner, rooting for me.

I'll try to remember that the next time she gets on my nerves.

CHAPTER 34

TONIGHT IS DEFINITELY ANOTHER Little Black Dress night. But this time, it has nothing to do with a man.

It's all about a menu.

Dr. Liz and I decide our last night in Paris would be our Big Splurge. We look for a restaurant with the highest number of Michelin Stars we can find.

Épicure sounds perfect. A three-starred "temple of gastronomy" located in Le Bristol Paris, a swanky hotel on the ultrafancy Rue du Faubourg. Forget Sancerre: tonight cries out for nothing less than a cold glass of Dom Pérignon champagne, and a warm, loving toast.

"To mothers and daughters everywhere," I say.

"Yes," she says. "And especially in Paris."

Clink.

"This is lovely," my mother says. It's a word she

rarely uses. But it's the perfect way to describe the champagne, the ambience, the menu. A rare occasion of the description living up to the hype.

I glance around. We're seated at a table overlooking the lush interior garden of Le Bristol. The room is filled with people who look like movers and shakers, most of them French, and all assumedly with deep pockets. But there's a total lack of haughtiness. Everyone is here for a wonderful meal, a genteel evening, a gracious night on the town.

Our two waiters come over and introduce themselves. Yes, two: one for each guest at the table, according to what I read online. Robert (pronounced Ro-*bear*) is in his late twenties, tall and slim with a lot of dark hair and the perfect amount of facial scruff. He looks a little like Ro-*bear* Pattinson. Moran, our second waiter, is older, shorter, and gray-haired. The word that comes to mind is *distingué*. Distinguished. Like a matinee idol of the 1930s.

They describe this evening's prix-fixe menu: duck foie gras; stuffed macaroni with black truffles and artichokes; langoustines cooked with lemon thyme and coriander; potatoes mousseline smoked with haddock; and for the finale, chocolate with lemon foam.

Luckily, my mother's cardiologist is nowhere in sight.

Dr. Liz looks especially beautiful this evening in a black beaded cashmere sweater, a pencil-thin silk skirt, and high heeled Louboutins. Even in our fanciest clothes we are just this side of underdressed, but that's okay. We both—yes, myself included—look smashing. Robert and Moran seem to notice. They are unnecessarily attentive.

Antoine, the serious, earthy, darkly handsome sommelier, also appears at our table. He offers a few suggestions, addressing all his comments to my mother. Once again, I see that flirtatious side of her as she bats her eyelashes and asks a question about the vintage, which I know for a fact she couldn't care less about.

"I think he likes you," I tell her as Antoine walks away.

"Nonsense," she says. "But that's sweet of you to say."

"I mean it. Who knew you were God's gift to men?"

She laughs. "I certainly didn't. But French men are just so . . . *out there*. Don't you think?"

"If you mean they don't play games, yes," I say.

"Women, sex, love—it's all so natural to them."

A little bell goes off in my head. This is the moment I've been waiting for.

"Does Dr. Beux fall into that category?" I ask.

She puts her glass down. "I was wondering when you were going to ask about him," she says. "No. I didn't have sex with him. Yes, he suggested it. But I didn't think it would be wise to get involved with a man who's a friend of my daughter. And I did *not* want to take a 'walk of shame' back to the hotel, thank you."

Voilà. Mystery solved. And all it took was one glass of champagne.

"He's a nice man," she says. "I'm sure he'll find someone else if he follows my advice."

"Which was—"

"To stop sending out all those needy vibes."

"But suppose a man—or woman—really *is* needy?"

She shrugs. She doesn't know what to advise someone like that. Neediness is totally off her radar.

The sommelier is back, showing my mother a bottle of Puligny-Montrachet wrapped in a napkin. He uncorks it and pours her a taste.

"Very nice," she says. He smiles as if he had stomped the grapes himself.

"For a very nice lady," he says, and pours us both glasses. Then he's gone.

"No word from Richard yet?" she asks.

A tiny pinprick of disappointment lodges in my chest. I try to ignore it. "No," I say. It comes out sadder than I would have hoped.

"Well, don't beat yourself up about it. You're a single woman in Paris! I can see how a little fling might have been hard to resist."

"Maybe it's genetic," I say. She laughs.

"Besides, there are plenty of other fish in the sea," she says. "Or as the French say, *Un de perdu, dix de retrouvés.* One lost, ten found."

"It's a nice idea," I say, "but I'm not finding *any*."

Our waiters come by with the first course: the pâté.

"What about *him*?" my mother says as they walk away.

"Who? Ro-*bear*?"

"Yes."

"No," I say, scooping some pâté onto a cracker. "Of the two, I think I'd be more into Moran."

"Personally," my mother says. "I would prefer Ro-*bear*...if I were twenty years younger."

Twenty? Not forty? Next, she'll be suggesting we double-date.

Across the room, Antoine the sommelier is making suggestions to another couple. But I notice he keeps stealing glances at my mother.

"You could probably go home with Antoine tonight," I say.

"No, not my type."

"You're practically seventy...and you still have a type?"

"See how you feel when *you're* seventy," she says, laughing. Meanwhile, she canvases the room for other possibilities. Before I realize what's happening, we've begun to play a mother-daughter version of the Netflix show, *Never Have I Ever.*

She gestures to a couple in their sixties. "That man in the navy blazer," she says. The man—silver haired, glasses—seems to make the woman he's with laugh every time he says something. "He looks like he'd be good in bed."

"Mother!"

"Don't look at me like that," she says. "I know all about these things."

"Yes but... you're my mother."

"When you were a teenager, your friends always used to ask me questions. Some of them—good lord! But you never did."

"Let me say it again: *you're my mother*."

"Now that one over there..." She points to a jowly hangdog-looking man scanning the menu. "I bet he's surprisingly exciting and tender."

"I can't believe we're talking like this."

"Your turn," she says.

I swivel my chair around to get a better view of the diners. I see a table of men at what looks like an expense-account dinner. One—early forties, dark hair, glasses—is a dead ringer for Clark Kent. I nod my head in Superman's direction.

My mother puts on her distance glasses and makes a face. "Really, Laurie?"

"I like his look. Serious and thoughtful."

"Synonyms for *dull*. You can do better."

More wine, more delicious food, and we can't seem to stop rating every man in the restaurant, even the ones lovingly draped over other women. We're giggling like two lovesick teenagers.

The balding man in the corner table?

"To come to a place like this alone?" my mother says. "That shows great self-confidence and stamina."

A truly stunning surfer dude with a blond ponytail at the other end of the room?

"All he *is* is handsome. You'd be bored by breakfast."

I pick my top five, with Clark Kent still in the lead. Dr. Liz picks her top five, including two new customers who've just walked in: both a bearded man with twinkly blue eyes, and—God help me!—his teenage son.

We order two cognacs to pair with the after-dinner truffles that they bring along with the check. She pays without letting me look at the amount. For all I know, she has written a love-note on it to Ro-*bear*. Or maybe her phone number.

A terrific evening. We leave the restaurant, both of us a little tipsy, and grab a cab. Once inside, she peers at the driver. She's still playing the game, scoping him out as a potential lover. "A definite maybe."

Never have I ever have known my mother had this fun, bawdy side.

And *never have I ever* have suspected she'd turn so horrible in just a few hours.

CHAPTER 35

THOUGHT FOR THE DAY: *No Good Deed Goes Unpunished.*

I was planning a surprise for my mother. I thought she'd love it. Boy, was I wrong.

Right before we left New York, I went on Ancestry .com and dug up contact info for her Norwegian relatives. I had to wade through lists of ancestors and cousins once, twice, three times removed till I found what I was looking for: Jeannie Ormson, the sister my mother hadn't seen or heard from in nearly fifty years, except for an annual Christmas card. I always thought that was odd, and for a while, I would ask my mother why. But she was always so evasive about it that I finally gave up.

I googled Jeannie. I could see the resemblance. Jeannie looks like what my mother would have looked like without hair color, portion control, and Pilates. She still lives in Kongsvinger, the town where they grew up, with her husband, Tore Hamre. He runs a small farm in the nearby countryside, and they've lived in the same place since they were married. They have three children: two married with children of their own, and one who lives in Copenhagen.

I emailed Jeannie to introduce myself and told her that my mother and I would be in Norway and wondered if we could stop by. She seemed thrilled. I gave her the dates of our trip and asked for directions from Oslo. *Do we need a car? Should we fly? Is there a train?*

She wrote back a long chatty email about how nice it would be to see her sister again after all these years. I told her we'd be in touch.

When I told my mother this morning, it was like setting off a keg of dynamite.

"*You . . . did . . . what?*" she yells.

"I wrote to your sister Jeannie and told her we were going to be in . . ."

"*How could you do that?!*" she screams. "*Behind my back!?*"

The bawdy, funny lady from last night has suddenly turned into the Dybbuk. Any moment now I'll see flames come shooting out of her mouth.

You had no right!

Without asking me?

What on earth made you think I'd ever want to see her again?

Now you've ruined everything!

Bottom line: not only is she not going to Kongsvinger with me, she's not going to Norway at all. *Not after this!*

My mother begins pulling all her clothes out of the closet and throwing them into her suitcase. Then she locks herself in the bathroom. Do I hear sniffles? Sobs? I'm not sure. When she comes out, she leaves the hotel room, slamming the door behind her.

I'm still sitting there, amazed. *What did I do wrong?*

I give her a few minutes, then go downstairs, hoping to find her cooling off in the lobby. She's not here.

I take a walk outside, a long final walk on our last day here. Past the heartbreaking ruins of Notre Dame, past the breathtaking stained-glass elegance of Sainte-Chapelle. And there it is: that little street with the chocolate shops from our very first day here.

Final Thought for the Day: There are few things in life that a couple of raspberry crème-filled truffles, deep dark chocolate ganaches, and chocolate hand-dipped orange slices can't fix.

CHAPTER 36

MY MOTHER IS BACK in the room when I return. I worry she's going to start screaming again. But no.

Her bags are packed. I start packing my bag as well. When I look up, I see she's holding a small package wrapped with brown paper and string.

"This is for you," she says quietly. "It's something I found at one of the bouquinistes."

I open it. It's a lithograph of a mother with her young daughter sitting on her lap. The mother is looking at the girl very tenderly. I feel myself welling up with tears.

"I am sorry for the way I acted before," my mother apologizes.

"No, I'm sorry," I say. "I never intended to upset you."

"I know." She seems tired. I think the argument took a lot out of her.

Her suitcases are lined up in front of the door.

"Does this mean you will be going to Norway after

all? I mean, I'm going, no matter what. But if you'd rather skip it—"

"I've thought about it," she says. "I will go. It will be nice to see the place again."

I'm not sure what she means by "the place." The house she was brought up in? The town where she was born? The country of Norway? I decide to leave well enough alone. I'm treading on eggshells here. So I just nod and continue packing.

"Should we ask the concierge to get us a car to the airport?" I say when I am finished.

Our flight isn't for a few hours, but we have no idea what the traffic or the check-in will be like.

"Yes," she says quietly. I know there's more to be said. A lot more. *I still don't understand any of this.*

When we get downstairs, a car is waiting for us. But so is something else.

The man behind the check-out desk hands me a handwritten note. "This was left for you early this morning," he says.

Laurie—

I'm back.

Can't tell you how many times I've thought about you the last few days.

Must see you again to figure out the hold you have on me.

Dinner tonight? Tomorrow?
Don't make me wait a minute longer than absolutely necessary…

Richard

CHAPTER 37

I WOULD'VE THOUGHT THAT offering to take my mother on a trip to cheer her up would have earned me some serious karma points.

Guess I was wrong.

I'm about to board a plane that will take me a thousand miles away from the man who came back to Paris to see me. I'm trying very hard not to be sad.

But the more we texted, the sadder I got:

ME: Dinner? Wish I could. On my way to Oslo.

Timing is everything, right?

HIM: Oh, no!!! How could this have happened? MY BAD for not getting in touch sooner. Long story. Too long for a text.

ME: ok

HIM: No, NOT ok. My heart is breaking. What's in Oslo (besides NOT ME)?

ME: Taking my mother back to explore her roots.

HIM: And after? Coming back to Paris, I hope. Or even better: London?

ME: Nope. Bergen, the Arctic Circle, a bunch of small towns...then home.

HIM: Oh dear. What shall i do here without u?

I would share this with my mother—along with the sweeter texts I exchanged yesterday with Françoise, who thanked me again for helping her home safely that night, and wanting to make sure Dr. Liz was feeling better—but her mood is not what you'd call receptive. She's grumbling again. Not about Norway. This time about our accommodations once we get there. I should have known that a woman used to upscale luxury hotels would balk at the very idea of an Airbnb.

"So let me make sure I understand," she says. "We're going to be staying in an apartment."

"Right."

"That belongs to a total stranger?"

"Yes," I say.

"We're going to be living in someone else's filth."

I knew this would be her major concern. So I'd carefully researched every apartment before sending in a deposit on a penthouse apartment at 18 Skovveien Street with all five-star cleanliness ratings. And most of the comments were in caps.

"SPARKLING clean!"—Veronika H, Asheville

"BETTER THAN NEW!"—Wendy W, Sebastopol

"TOTALLY spotless! And I'm a TOTAL CLEAN FREAK!"—Barbara H, Nantucket

My mother is still not sold. An apartment means no room service, no maid service, and no doorman.

"What's the neighborhood like?" she asks. "Is it safe? Will we be able to go out late at night?"

"We're right across from the Royal Palace," I say. I'm tempted to add, *if it's good enough for the King of Norway, it's good enough for you.* But thinking of her recent meltdown, I decide against it.

"Tell me again why we're doing this?" she demands.

"I thought it would be more interesting. We can experience the city like a native."

She looks at me and makes a face. "I *am* a native."

"Of Kongsvinger. Not of Oslo."

"Laurie . . ."

She's too annoyed to finish her sentence. But it turns out I was right. The apartment is spectacular. Bright and airy, with floor-to-ceiling windows that look out on a golden setting sun. It's almost twilight when we arrive. Distant city lights are beginning to twinkle. My mother examines the rooms, obviously pleased but determined not to give me the satisfaction.

MEAN THOUGHT: *I should have let her fly back to America when she threatened to.*

Or would that have made my karma even worse? I'm not sure. Instead, I suggest we take a walk.

Oslo, the capital of Norway, turns out to be

delightfully modern and cosmopolitan. All the women we pass look like my mother: tall stately blondes with great posture. It's like a convention of former ballerinas.

If all these beautiful blond women were put in a police lineup, I'm not sure I could identify Dr. Liz.

Another thing they have in common: their attitude. They carry themselves in a way that says they're proud to be here, proud to be Norwegian, proud to be who they are. My mother fits right in.

As for me, I can't seem to shake the disappointment I feel over just missing Richard. I try to keep it from my mother. But she senses something's off.

"What is it?" she asks.

I tell her about Richard's note and our subsequent flurry of texts.

"I'm sorry," she says, surprisingly sympathetic. Then she adds, cryptically, "You know, sometimes the universe is trying to tell you something."

I wonder what that might be. I'm thinking of all those inspirational verses on greeting cards: how people come into your life for a season or a reason, and sometimes they leave footprints on your heart.

But none of them mentions being kicked in the teeth.

CHAPTER 38

EVERYTHING I EVER NEEDED to understand about my mother becomes clear the moment I step into the Viking Ship Museum:

My mother is descended from Vikings.

Just inside the entrance is the Oseberg ship, an authentic seventy-six-foot-long Viking vessel.

I can picture Dr. Liz standing at the helm, telescope raised, staring off in the direction of dry land and barking orders to the thirty oarsmen behind her. "Row faster. Faster. *Faster.*"

Thomas Galvin, the museum docent, is here to answer all our questions in English, which I quickly learn just about every Norwegian speaks. We don't have a lot of them. But the museum is relatively empty, and Tom is anxious to share what he knows about ninth-century Norway. He's so sincere, we don't want to hurt his feelings. But I can't stop thinking about Richard.

"The ship is made of pine and oak," he says, "with iron rivets. Those rich carvings of animals and serpent's heads indicate the Oseberg ship was probably made for Viking aristocracy." My mother's ancestors?

I'm trying hard to stifle a yawn as Tom describes the Oseberg excavation in 1904. I perk up when he mentions that archeologists discovered it had been used as a burial chamber. Inside, they found the remains of two women, possibly a mother and daughter.

My mother and I look at each other and laugh. Can you imagine? The two of us, buried together for eternity?

"It could have been a wealthy woman and her servant," Tom hedges. "Or two sisters, both laid to rest on a bed of linen."

But we decide we like his mother-daughter possibility best. Especially when we hear what was buried with them:

Clothes, shoes, and combs (sounds like us)

Ship's equipment (eh, doesn't sound like us)

Kitchen utensils (hmmm...maybe)

Farm tools (definitely not us)

Three ornate sleighs and one working sleigh (yes: three for her, one for me)

A cart (ME: "I bet the mother made her pull it." DR. LIZ: "Don't be fresh.")

Five beds (my mother would get first dibs)

Two tents (for when they argued)

After the museum, we head to the Vigeland Park. Two hundred bronze, granite, and wrought-iron sculptures donated to the city by the artist Gustav Vigeland—all of them nude. A naked man laughing as he lifts a naked woman over his head.

(Reminds me of Richard.) A naked man seated on a pedestal, lost in thought. (Reminds me of Richard.) A naked man holding up a bunch of babies as if they were bananas. (Reminds me of...well, you get the picture.)

There are several elementary school groups milling around. The kids are stifling giggles as the boys point to various granite genitalia.

"I don't think this would be considered a G-rated school trip in America," I say.

My mother agrees. "Back home, this would never fly," she says. "Norwegians have a much healthier attitude toward the human body."

I'm thinking of my own childhood. In fifth grade, my school offered an elective sex education class. But you weren't allowed to take it unless your parent signed a permission slip.

Needless to say, Dr. Liz signed. I was just glad she didn't ask to *teach* it.

When I went off to college, my mother was the one who suggested I go on birth control pills. I always knew she was more comfortable talking about sex than I was. Now I know where she got it from.

Our last stop for the afternoon: the massive Holmenkollen Tower, site of the 1952 Olympics ski jump. When we get out of the cab, my mother looks at it and smiles. More memories? *Yes.*

"My parents brought us here when we were little," she says.

"To ski?" I ask, horrified.

"Certainly not," she says, laughing. "We brought sleds to slide down the bottom part. In summer, we'd walk up as high as we could and then roll down. My father took home movies. I wonder if my sister still has them."

We shade our eyes and peer up to the very top. Several people are sliding down the Kollensvevet zip line, which takes you from the top of the tower all the way to the bottom at the same speed as if you were on skis.

"My parents always promised we could do that someday," says Dr. Liz, watching them. "But we never did. And then I moved to America."

I hope she's not thinking what I think she's thinking.

"I've always wondered how it would feel..." she says.

"No!" I say.

"...to go whizzing by at that speed."

I look at her with alarm. "You can't mean...?"

"C'mon," she says, handing me her purse to hold. "Don't be such a Debbie Downer. What's the worst that can happen?"

The worst? She could break an arm or a leg or a hip, in which case I would have to get her to an Oslo hospital, with no Françoise here to smooth the way.

The *very* worst? She could have another heart attack and die here, and I'd have to find a way to . . .

Wait a minute: didn't I have this exact anxiety attack earlier, when we were still in Paris? Yes. It's all coming back to me. It's what a friend of mine calls *déjà vu revisited*.

"I don't think that's such a good idea," I say.

"Try and stop me," she says. I know I can't.

Instead, I wait at the foot of the ski jump as she buys a ticket and takes the elevator up to the top of the jump tower. I watch as they strap her into the zip line harness. She waves. Then she grabs on to the support poles and soars down over the city at God-knows-how-many miles per hour, smiling all the way.

The guidebooks describe the Kollensvevet zip line as 361 meters of *pure pounding adrenaline*. And it is.

Not hers. *Mine*.

CHAPTER 39

IF I EVER MADE a needlepoint pillow for my mother, I know what it would say:

"*En dag uten shopping er som en dag uten solskinn.*"

"A day without shopping is like a day without sunshine."

The next morning, I am up bright and early. But not as early as my mother. By the time I roll out of bed, she has set the table with breakfast from a local *Dagligvarebutikk* (grocery store), which we picked up on the way back to the apartment last night: berries, bread, boysenberry jam, smoked salmon, yogurt, pick-led herring, and *brunost,* a crumbly brown cheese she hopes I will like.

I don't. It smells like old socks.

While I was still asleep, she even began preparing tomorrow's breakfast: *øllebrød,* a porridge made with pieces of dry rye bread soaked in beer for twenty-four hours, then served with milk, raisins, and orange zest. It smells delicious, but I'm surprised. I've never seen her cook Norwegian food before in my life. I'd always assumed she'd forgotten how. But maybe she just never *wanted* to. A reminder of a life she wanted to forget.

As we eat, Dr. Liz is delighted to learn that Frogner, the area right behind the Royal Palace, is one of the best shopping districts in the city. Rather than waste a minute, we leave our dirty dishes in the sink and head out. She can't wait to get started.

"Here's a quiz for you," I say as we enter the first shop. "What's the main difference between this store and most of the ones we know back home?"

She looks around and thinks.

"A lack of clutter," she says. Good for her. She got it on the first try. I'm used to stores cramming things onto rods or stacking them up to the ceiling. But Norwegians like to give their wares room to breathe. A few simple sweatshirts sit on a glass shelf. A bunch of hand-knit fisherman sweaters hang from a pole, three inches apart.

"In Norway, it seems you're encouraged to browse, not just buy," my mother says. "It's like they want shopping to be more relaxed and fun." Need I add, she's determined to have all the fun she can today. My mother intends to hit every clothing, furniture, and craft shop from here down to the harbor, and she doesn't want a slowpoke like me to cramp her style.

So we split up. As she disappears into the next shop, my phone buzzes. It's a new text from Richard:

Alone in Paris. DAY TWO of the hostage crisis...?

I can't decide whether to laugh or cry. Maybe a little retail therapy *will* distract me. I wander over to the sweater rack.

"Lovely, aren't they?" the salesgirl says to me in English. She introduces herself as Ingrid. "They're all hand-made by Christl Riple, a marvelous knitter right here in town. Aren't they wonderful?" She's right. They are. And they're all one-of-a-kind in shades of red, forest green, and navy blue.

I pull out a red-and-white one filled with eight-pointed stars, snowflakes, and hundreds of red-and-white diamonds and squares. It fits me like a dream. I can't resist. *My first official Norwegian souvenir purchase.* Dr. Liz will be pleased.

I continue down the street, hoping to spot my mother at some point. But she's probably holed up in a dressing room somewhere, so I don't see her. My next purchase: a navy-and-white hand knit scarf with a Viking ship that extends from one end of the scarf all the way to the other. And, of course, a pair of matching mittens.

Now I come to the most crucial part of any travel shopping trip: The Search For The Perfect Keychain. I've been collecting them for as long as I can remember, one for every city I visit. Naturally, I bought a mini-Eiffel-Tower one in Paris at a souvenir shop around the corner from our hotel. I'd love to find a less cliché one here, and already I see several that look good to me. But as I said, this is a crucial decision. Do I want a Viking ship? A moose? A moose whose mouth doubles as a bottle opener? A map of Norway?

In the end, I opt for a copper-colored reindeer. As I'm paying, my mother passes by the store window, sees me inside, and taps on glass. She gestures for me to come outside. So I do.

She's smiling. "Here," she says. She hands me a small pink box with a magenta ribbon. The box says *Hilde's Jewelry Studio.*

"For me?" I ask stupidly. "Why?"

"I know how upset you are by that whole Richard fiasco," she says. "I thought this might cheer you up a little."

How sweet!

"You'd like the shop. Very arty. Hilde makes all of the pieces herself." Then she says the eight magic words that made me miserable throughout my childhood: "I thought you would look good in this."

This time, *I'm* the one whose memories come flooding back.

I thought you would look good in an ugly blouse that made a chubby middle-schooler look even chubbier.

I thought you would look good in a pair of clunky

old-lady shoes because the sneakers I loved didn't give me enough arch support.

I thought you would look good in a multitude of tops, bottoms, and dresses, each more hideous than the last. Saying no started an argument that always ended with the totally ego-crushing, *"You don't know what looks good on you."*

Just for the record: *none* of them ever looked good on me.

So when she hands me the box now, I am flummoxed. Her intentions are good. It's something she handpicked. *To cheer you up,* she said. But what if it's ugly? Will I have to wear it every time I see her? Is it something expensive, or can I donate it to Goodwill the day I get back home?

But: surprise. It's a pair of sterling earrings, classic Norwegian filigree design, with a playful modern twist. They are delicate and feminine. Exactly how I would love to think of myself, but rarely do.

She smiles. "I had a feeling you would like these."

I take out the studs I am currently wearing and slide these in instead. She pulls out her hand mirror and holds it up to my face. I shake my head a little. The earrings sway and gently graze the top of my shoulders. They look great.

"Thank you," I say.

So that's how we end this shopping day. No arguing. No angst. No disapproving looks or name-calling or anger to tamp down and resent. Nothing but a loving mother picking out a lovely gift for her grateful daughter.

I guess over the years, one of us has matured and the other has mellowed.

Hard to say which is which.

CHAPTER 40

FOR OUR LAST-NIGHT SPLURGE in Oslo, I choose a restaurant called Kontrast with a tasting menu that sounds phenomenal. It's all the way on the other side of the city, a half-hour cab ride away.

From the simple stucco facade outside, I wonder if I have made a mistake.

Then we step inside. Now I'm sure I made a mistake.

The interior is stark. A concrete floor and exposed pipework give it an industrial edge that's a world away from the kind of *last-night splurge* we had in Paris and were hoping for again tonight.

It's plain, blunt, unadorned. No tablecloths. No chandeliers. A single flower in a bud vase on each of only eight occupied tables, all spaced widely apart. No luxury decor touches anywhere. My mother looks around, disappointed.

But it turns out all the grand ruffles and flourishes have been saved for the food.

The first nice touch: a busboy brings over a small bench for our purses.

Then we look at tonight's tasting menu. It's filled with magical names and ingredients that neither of us have heard of.

"What's *Chawanmushi*?" my mother asks.

"I bet that's some guru the chef follows."

She smiles.

I'm wrong, of course. *Chawanmushi* turns out to be a Japanese soft egg custard made with smoked haddock. But at least my mother is smiling.

"Asparagus with fir shoots?" she asks.

"A fir is a kind of tree, like a Christmas tree," I say. "So it's probably puréed needles."

This is the kind of fun wordplay and banter we do back at the advertising agency—something my mother has never been privy to. I'm on a roll.

"And look at this," she says. "Fried mink whale."

"Well, sure," I say. "Even fur tastes good when it's fried."

Now she's laughing. We settle down once the food arrives.

Kontrast believes in combining different colors, flavors, and textures to create unique taste sensations. And it works. Shelf flower sauce? Birch syrup? Oxidized sunflower seeds? We may not know what any of it is. But we know it all tastes wonderful.

By the time we're finished with our meal and sipping coffee, I am feeling sated and happy. Tomorrow I will have a dreadful food-and-drink hangover. But every last bite tonight has been worth it.

And then my phone buzzes.

I turned the ringer off, but it's still on vibrate. I might not even have noticed it, except the little bench shudders a bit. I look at it.

It's another text from Richard.

Couldn't resist. I'm here in Oslo. The Hotel Continental.

Meet me? Tonight? Right now? Sooner?

My mother notices the look of shock on my face. She expects the worst.

"Something wrong?"

"No. It's, uh, Richard. He's, um, here. In Oslo."

"Oh," she says. It's definitely an "oh" laden with meaning. But I don't pursue it.

"He wants me to meet him at his hotel."

Pause. "When?"

Another pause. "Um . . . now?"

Like me, she is trying to process this. He followed me all the way to Oslo. Is that magically romantic, or too outrageous to consider normal? Is he caring, compulsive, or just plain crazy? What do I know about him, really? What should I do?

The two of us sit silently for a moment, sipping our coffee, trying to sort it all out.

She speaks first. "Go to him," she says at last.

"Really?"

"I'll have the mâitre d' call me a cab," she says. "Make sure you text me when you get there."

I stand up. I kiss her goodbye, and wonder if I should lighten the moment by asking her the most pressing question:

Can I still keep the earrings?

CHAPTER 41

I'M ALONE IN THE taxicab on my way to Richard's hotel, playing a game I just invented. It's called Think Like a Mother. Tonight, the parts of both the mother and the daughter are being played by... me.

MOTHER: Laurie, why have you agreed to meet this guy?

ME: How could I not? The man has flown a thousand miles to see me. That must mean something.

MOTHER: Such as?

ME: That he's romantic. And that he really likes me.

MOTHER: Well, if you ask me, he sounds like a stalker.

ME: I *didn't* ask you. And why is it so hard for you to believe he actually cares for me? Besides, *I* like *him*. He's charming and adorable, with the kind of little-boy innocence no woman could resist, and...

Suddenly I realize: I am describing both Richard and Ted Bundy.

Oh, God. What if my mother is right?

(PAUSE game, as contestant wonders if she should proceed to the next level or ask the cab driver to turn around.)

By the time I exit the taxi at the very grand Hotel Continental, I've worked myself into quite a state. My heart is racing from all the adrenaline, excitement, and fear bubbling around inside me, fighting for space.

Just to be on the safe side, I make it a point to say hello to the woman behind the registration desk and double-check Richard's room number. That way she'll be able to tell the police that yes, a woman of my description arrived around ten fifteen. *But no, we never saw her leave. But we did see the man she was visiting exit some time later, struggling under the weight of a large rolled-up rug.*

See, that's the thing about a good imagination. It can be your best friend. Or, in times like this, your worst enemy. As I take the elevator up, I keep going back and forth in my mind: Murderer? Seducer? Lover? Solicitor? Killer? All of the above? I hold my breath as I knock on his door.

And there he is.

That great wavy salt-and-pepper hair. The same sweet crooked little smile. The same hug, except that this one seems to go on for much longer than any of the others.

So far, so good.

He's wearing a handsome striped shirt, untucked. After our hug, he stands back and looks at me. Then he gives me a chaste kiss on the cheek.

"You're looking...well, uh...*well*," he says last, stammering a bit. As usual, he's a tad unsure of himself when he speaks. "I was afraid..."

"What?" I ask.

"That you wouldn't be as lovely as I remember," he says shyly. But then he shakes his head. "No. The actual truth is...I was afraid, um, that you wouldn't show up."

And now I remember something: one of the delights of this man is how honest and unsure of himself he is. *Too bad he's not a litigator. He'd have every woman on the jury totally smitten.*

"And you," I say, channeling my mother, "are crazy."

"Why do you say that?"

"Following me from a thousand miles away?"

"My good woman, I'll have you know, I had no choice. I had to track you down. I missed you." He leans over and kisses me again.

All the wine I had at dinner has made me somewhat gutsier than usual. So I say what's on my mind. "And yet you waited three days to get in touch?"

He's silent for a moment. "I was planning to," he confesses. "But...I needed to get my ducks in a row."

He needed to be prepared before sending a text?

Does he mean his legal ducks or his emotional ducks? I'm not sure. But I let it go.

"But now that I'm here…" He leans over to kiss me. A real kiss this time. Then slowly, gently, we start undressing one another. His Turnbull & Asser tie, my silk blouse, his Savile Row bespoke shirt, my Wacoal bra, one piece and one kiss at a time.

We make love slowly, with giggles all along the way. He is a gentle romantic lover who takes his time and makes every moment count. And if he notices the some-what rounder body that I have been feeding with French truffles and Big Splurge dinners since he left…he is enough of a gentleman not to say anything.

Afterward, I put my head on his shoulder and we talk.

"Did you really travel all the way to Oslo just to see me?" I ask.

"Why are you so surprised?" he says. "I told you I'd be back."

Right. And if I had a nickel for every man who ever said that to a woman…

"I thought about you the whole entire time I was gone," he says.

"Pining away?"

"Pretty much so. A chance meeting with lovely lady. How unexpected life can sometimes be."

It feels good to have a man say such nice things to me. It's been a while, but I don't tell him that.

"And how is Mum? Treating you all right, I gather."

I tell him about the zip line adventure, and he laughs. But when I tell him about her meltdown, he looks concerned.

"Hmmm," he says. But it's a *hmmm* filled with subtext. "Sounds a tad dodgy, for the kind of woman you've been describing."

"Which is what?"

"Like Lady Macbeth, if she'd gone to medical school," he says. "My guess would be she's hiding something."

He might be right. But thinking about my mother is the last thing I want to do right now.

We make love again and it is just as grand. Then afterward he turns to me and says, "I never thought I could feel this way again about a woman."

Again? The word jumps out at me. But why am I so surprised? Of course he has a history. Everybody does.

"How long will you be here?" I ask.

"That depends. How long are you staying?"

"Uh . . . actually, we're leaving for Bergen tomorrow."

"Brilliant," he says, shaking his head. "I guess I should have asked about your itinerary." He thinks for a moment. Then he adds, "I can join you. That is, if I wouldn't be in the way."

In the way? How sweet.

"I should tell you: we're taking the train. It's a seven-hour journey."

"Oh. Well, lovely as it would be to sit across from

you and your mum for seven hours…um, would it be all right if I just met you there?"

"Of course."

I look at the clock. I haven't gotten much sleep. But I can sleep on the train. All I need to do now is dress, take a cab back to our hotel, shower, pack, and head to the train station.

Oh—and at some point, mention to my mother that I have invited a plus-one.

CHAPTER 42

SEVEN HOURS ON A train with my mother.

Actually, it's not as terrible as it sounds.

We bought a few Norwegian delicacies at the Oslo station before we left: some *fiskebollar* (fish balls) and *rakfisk* (fillets of trout) to put on the *lefse* (soft bread), as well as cheeses and sweets and bottled water. With fifteen minutes to kill before boarding, I suggest we poke around a wine store and buy a bottle.

"It's a little early to be drinking, don't you think?" she asks.

"It's for later," I say. "We'll open it as soon as the fjords come into view." She grudgingly agrees.

There are lots of great-looking, great-sounding European wines and vintages on the shelf. But one label jumps out at us. A California Sangiovese, Love You Bunches. The name makes us smile. I buy a bottle.

With the help of two cheerful Norwegian porters,

we load all four of my mother's suitcases onto the train. She has way too much to fit in the overhead. So they stack her bags up on the metal rack in the back of the car. I carry my one duffel bag myself.

I'm hoping she'll let me have the window seat so I can catch up on my sleep. No such luck. Without asking, my mother slides in first.

I'm still waiting for her to ask me about last night. She barely alluded to it when I got back to the room at five in the morning. She was awake, of course. All she said was, "Finally." That's Dr. Liz–speak for: *I certainly couldn't fall asleep knowing my only daughter was alone with a veritable stranger in a foreign city.*

She leans against the window and closes her eyes. The rhythm of the train works its magic on her. In just a few minutes I hear her gentle ladylike snores. I look around. The car is not too crowded. A few people are engrossed in books. A few more are texting. The rest are chatting quietly with their seat mates.

I eat a cheese, trout, and *lefse* sandwich and think about last night. It makes me smile. Richard checks a lot of boxes: considerate, honest, not afraid to show his feelings. Besides the great chemistry between us, I *like* him. And I like who I am with him. He makes me feel good about myself. That alone is worth the price of admission.

The first hour of the ride is dreary. We pass through a huge industrial area of warehouses and factories: metal buildings, rusted metal signs, lots of telephone wires and parking lots. There's absolutely nothing charming about it. No wonder most of the other passengers have put down their electronic devices and closed their eyes.

Did I make a mistake? Should we have flown instead?

Soon, things begin to change.

As the factories disappear, I start to see country-side, farmhouses, small towns. Then thousands of trees blanketed in a gentle mist that reminds me of Heath-cliff's moors. We pass a small waterfall. Then rocks and greenery, a touch of snow on grass-covered hills, and melted ice patches on far-off mountains. This part of Norway feels like the inside of a snow globe. I'm not the only one noticing. Everyone who's awake is looking out the window, glued to the landscape.

My mother is still sleeping. So I decide to stretch my legs a bit. A few rows down is a group of six women seated across from one another. They look like they range in age from eighteen to seventy. Ever since we boarded, I've noticed how well they get along, laughing and chatting gaily. Are they mothers and daughters? I doubt it. I'm curious. I walk over to them.

"Excuse me," I say. "I was just wondering: are you all related?"

They seem quite happy that someone has taken an interest in them.

"Goodness no," says one of the women. "Well, Frida

here is my mother." She puts her arm around a gray-haired lady next to her who says hello. "And I'm Hanne. The rest of us—well, we all just love to knit."

A knitting group. Of course.

"We do an annual trip together, twenty of us in all. This year we're meeting up with the others in Bergen."

She introduces Astrid, Grethe, Inger, and Hedda. As if on cue, they all lean over and pull out their knitting bags to show me what they're working on. It's a dazzling display of patterns and stitches in unusual shades like orchid and magenta. Inger holds up a tiny half-finished pink sweater knitted with little black-and-white Elmos. "For my brand new *barnebarn,*" she says proudly.

"Now show her what you made last month for Enok," Hanne says. They all giggle as Inger hands me her cell phone.

Enok, it turns out, is a German shepherd. He's posing for the camera wearing a beautiful brown-and-beige Norwegian dog sweater. His mouth is open so wide, I'd swear he's smiling.

"I want you all to see something," I say. I head back to my duffel bag and pull out the sweater I bought in Oslo.

"What do you think?" I ask Hanne.

She cradles it in her hands as if it's a newborn baby and looks at it lovingly, turning it inside out, checking the stitches.

"This is a beauty," she says. "Do you know who made it?"

"Christl Riple, the salesgirl told me."

"Christl! We love her work!" says Hedda. It turns out Christl is kind of a superstar in the Norwegian knitting world. She's even lectured at some of their meetings.

The sweater has made its rounds all the way down to Grethe, who's seated at the end. "I know this pattern!" she says. She's very excited, like a contestant on a quiz show. "This is from Innsbruck 1976! It was designed for the Winter Olympics."

"Quite a wonderful piece you have there," Hanne says, handing it back to me. "Not just beautiful, but a little piece of history. Wear it in good health."

"Thank you," I say. I wish them all well and head back to my seat just as my mother is waking up. I tell her about the knitting group. Dr. Liz is a serious antique collector who always insists on knowing the provenance of everything she purchases. So I'm sure she'll be interested in what I learned about my sweater.

Wrong again.

"I never had the patience for knitting," she says. Then she closes her eyes and sleeps for another hour.

CHAPTER 43

THE GUIDEBOOKS SAY THE fjords were formed by thousands of glaciers slowly melting over millions of years. As our train swerves to the left, they come into view. You can see how it would take millions of years to create something this incredible.

Or not.

Nothing like a breathtaking, magnificent, overwhelming spectacle to get the creative juices flowing. Maybe even overflowing. So with several hours ahead of me, I start crafting a whole new scenario in my head. Let's call it "Laurie's Story of How the Fjords Were Born." (Maybe it's a children's book.)

Once upon a time, Mother Nature looked around and said, "Yes, this earth is quite beautiful. But is it *beautiful enough*?"

Naturally, there was no one around to ask.

So Mother Nature made an executive decision: she cracked the earth open and filled the spaces with roaring rivers, gentle lakes, and waterfalls in all the blue shades of the rainbow, from soft aquamarine to stunning sapphire.

But, wait. There was a problem. Now the earth looked too much like spring.

"I know," Mother Nature said. "I'll turn that jagged coastline into crystalline rock walls. And those spiky hills? Poof! Now they're snow-covered glaciers. *That* should make the world sit up and take notice."

And indeed, it has.

THE END

All around me, passengers are glued to the windows in awe. We see sheep meadows and fruit trees, farm landscapes and tony little towns, frosty mountain peaks that sparkle in the sun. And now and then, a lone hiker. It's a glorious untamed wilderness of ice above and greenery below. No wonder everyone on the train gasps in wonder.

My mother reopens her eyes. That's my cue to open the wine.

"Love You Bunches," I say. My mother looks confused. Does she think I'm talking about us? Hardly. "The *wine*," I say, handing her a glass. "Remember?"

"Oh, right." Together we toast the towering cliffs of jagged rock on both sides of the water, glittering in the sunlight. No wonder they call this one of the great train rides in the world.

We're almost a little sad when the train winds into Bergen. Though the idea of seeing Richard again soon helps keep my spirits high.

Our hotel is right across the street from the train station. Turns out the location is the only good thing my mother can say about the place. Now that I changed her mind about Airbnbs, I decided to press my luck by picking a Bergen hotel that was low on stars but high on charm.

Big mistake.

The black metal chandeliers in the lobby look like giant iron spiders crawling along the ceiling. The lobby itself, done in shades of purple, violet, and black, looks like the setting for *Halloween III: Season of the Witch.* Even the people at the check-in desk seem creepy. In drab black uniforms, they look like Norwegian Munsters.

My mother is still too groggy to criticize me outright. Instead, she resorts to Dr. Liz–speak: "How did you ever get lucky enough to find a place like this?"

I decide to be honest. "I thought you might like a change from elegance."

She looks at me and laughs. She's right. This place looks like a Viking prison. *What was I thinking?*

It isn't just the lobby. It turns out that everything

about the Hotel Oleana is...quirky. The elevator is filled with neon panels that change colors as you move.

The elevator music? What else but the score from *Sweeney Todd,* about a homicidal barber who makes meat pies of his victims.

Our rooms, which are next door to one another, are just as peculiar. Mine has purple bathroom tiles and black walls, plus a tiny porthole window with a five-inch city view. I dread hearing what my mother has to say about hers.

I don't have to wait long.

By the time I return to the lobby, my mother is engaged in a not-quite-heated-but-pretty-close discussion with one of the Norwegian Munsters at the desk. My mother is frowning. As I get closer, I hear she's speaking in rapid-fire Norwegian, but I can make out the English words *coffin* and *crypt*. I try to convince myself that she's asking directions to some famous mausoleum. But—*who am I kidding?*—she's obviously complaining about the room. He says they'll move her to something more appropriate. She demands a suite. He looks at his supervisor, who says okay. She nods and walks away. I don't hear her say thank you.

It is late afternoon. Too early to eat. Instead, we head to Kaffekompaniet, a tiny Starbucks-like shop a short walk from the hotel. We order two cappuccino macadamias and a yummy apple pastry made by the owner's wife, who also makes mittens. Dozens of hand-knit pairs are draped around the shop like Christmas garlands. When my mother pulls out her credit card to pay for the coffee, she's like a gun-slinger with a twitchy trigger finger. She buys ten tiny pairs.

"For my next ten newborn babies," she says.

The coffee is good and strong. It perks us up. We decide to get tickets and board the Fløibanen, the local funicular ride to the top of Mount Fløyen, the highest point in Bergen. There aren't many other tourists—it's late in the day, late in the season. Our little metal car fills with locals heading up to the top for a drink, an early dinner, or maybe the city's best photo op. The ride passes through beautiful wild grasses and shrubbery. But as we get close to the top, it begins to rain. And our umbrellas are back in our rooms. *Walking around in the rain? What fun is that?*

A woman standing near us hears us talking and smiles.

"In Norway, we have a saying that will help you," she says. *"Det finnes ikke noe slikt som dårlig vær. Bare dårlige klær."*

My mother laughs.

"What does that mean?" I ask.

"There's no such thing as bad weather. Only bad clothes."

She's right, of course. When we get to the top of Mount Fløyen, we duck into a gift shop and buy two cheap plastic ponchos—one white, one black. It's hard to say which is uglier.

My mother puts her arm around me as we wander around. We pass a wooden sign that lists the distance to fifteen different cities—Beijing 7254 km, Berlin 1004 km. Naturally, we can't resist taking a selfie of the two of us pointing to the part that says New York 5623 km. We laugh when we see ourselves in the photos. The ponchos are even less flattering than we thought. We look like the Pillsbury Doughboy on a date with the Michelin Man.

"What do you want to do now?" I ask. "We could walk around a little bit more while it's still light out."

My mother shakes her head no. "I'd like to sit down. How about we just stop for ice cream?"

"What? And ruin our appetites?" I can't resist saying.

It's a caution she threw at me hundreds of times when I was a child. The real answer: "Nothing could ruin my appetite." But that would have led to a lecture about my weight.

My sarcasm seems to go over my mother's head, and that worries me. Yes, it's been a long day and we were up early to catch the train. But she's just not her usual self. It isn't just her lack of energy. Something is troubling her. The scariest symptom of all: she doesn't even have the strength to criticize.

Inside the gift shop again, we make our way past the T-shirts and souvenir coffee mugs to the ice cream counter. The Norwegian flavors sound irresistible. I try a White Chocolate Evergreen cone with a ribbon of Red Currant. It's wonderful; it tastes like Christmas. My mother opts for a Browned Butter cup with chunks of salty almond brittle. She proclaims it delicious but eats only half.

The rain is beginning to stop. "Should we walk around a little more now?" I ask.

She pauses. "I think I'd rather go back to the room," she says. "I'm a little . . . winded."

Uh-oh.

I keep forgetting she's a woman with a heart condition. I buy two funicular return tickets. We had talked about walking down the mountain on the way back, but that's off the table now.

Back at the hotel, I'm still feeling uneasy. Two days ago, my mother blithely sped down a zip line. Today, she seems to have trouble walking. If I bring it up, she will deny it vehemently and go out of her way to prove me wrong.

Then again, we *were* on the top of a mountain. Everybody knows the air is much thinner up there. Right?

Yes, of course. That must be it.

CHAPTER 44

MY MOTHER TAKES A nap before dinner. She's well rested now. So, of course, she starts complaining about the hotel.

"Did you know there's no dining room here?" she asks. "They make you eat breakfast in the *lobby*." She says the word *lobby* as if she's saying *gutter*.

"I know. But it's supposed to be great here. And it's only breakfast. Plus it's a good way to meet people."

"I know enough people," she says. It's true—back home her Rolodex is overflowing with people she's met in medical school, at hospitals, through charity work, from seminars, conventions, and her neighborhood. I assumed, like me, that she'd enjoy chatting with other travelers, certainly with some of her Norwegian brethren. Once again, I am wrong.

Bergen is an enchanting city at twilight. It looks like one of those impossibly picturesque miniature villages you see in store windows during Christmas. Tall colorful wooden townhouses built in the eleventh century stand gable-to-gable along the quay and all the way up the surrounding hill. Most have a shop on the lower level—leather goods, jewelry, pottery—and an apartment above. As we walk along the cobblestone streets, my mother's mood is improving. I'm sure it's because she's thinking of hitting all the stores tomorrow.

Dinner is at Bryggen Tracteursted, a charming eighteenth-century restaurant that resembles a chalet: thick wooden crossbeams on the ceiling and original oak floors. One sip of Hansa beer and Dr. Liz is back to her old self.

"So, tell me about last night," she says. *Well. Finally.*

"He's a nice guy," I say. "It was nice seeing him."

My mother looks at me and frowns. "That's it?"

I shrug.

"Laurie, you're in advertising. Surely you can come up with a better sell than that."

She's waiting to hear more. Dreading her judgments, I am not particularly forthcoming. Just then the waiter appears at our side. Timing is everything.

"Do you have any questions about the menu?" he asks.

I'm feeling adventurous. "Tell me about the reindeer," I say. "What's it like?"

"Most people expect it to be gamey, like venison.

It's not. It's leaner than beef, surprisingly mild and...
beef-like."

I think for a moment. "And what's *kattematt*?"

"Stewed cod cheeks with mussels."

Feeling—well, cheeky—I order both, one for an
appetizer, one for an entrée.

"And I'll have the salmon to start, and then the
lutefisk," my mother says, "with an order of *lefse*."

The waiter scribbles it down.

"Thank you, ladies."

I'm trying to think of something to prevent my
mother from returning to the topic of Richard.

"I didn't even know codfish *had* cheeks," I say.

"Don't change the subject," she says. Wise woman.

"All right." I take a deep breath. "I'm not in love with
him, if that's what you're worried about. He's a sweet
guy who seems...smitten."

"Obviously. No normal man would track you down
the way he did without being, as you say, smitten. I
could have told you that."

She obviously disapproves of...well, everything. I
can feel my blood start to boil. But I tamp it down
and speak.

"I'm just enjoying having somebody like Richard in
my life right now," I say. "He's good for me. Good for
my ego."

"And...?"

"And he reminds me of what's possible between a

man and a woman. Something I'd pretty much given up on since the fiasco with Andrew."

Our salmon and *kattemat* arrive. I taste it. It's rich with a nice bracing fennel flavor. And my reindeer is surprisingly tender and pleasant. So is the rest of our evening together.

Because I still haven't told her that Richard is on his way to join us.

CHAPTER 45

THE GREAT NORWEGIAN ARTIST Edvard Munch was not a happy camper.

My mother and I are at Kode 3, one of Bergen's modern art museums. It's a stone building with enormous floor-to-ceiling windows that look out over the sparkling city—a stark contrast to the highly depressing Munch exhibit inside.

Munch was a deeply troubled guy who suffered from a genetic mental condition, and it shows. All his paintings depict people crying out in psychic pain. In one, three generations of women (mother, grandmother, child) stand in the shadow of black-shrouded Death. In another, a cluster of townspeople dressed in black walks toward us, a parade of sadness and grief. We see a naked woman hugging a dead lover, another embracing a skeleton. And of course, you can't miss the pencil sketch for his most famous work, the truly suicidal *Scream*.

I was unprepared for the unrelenting despair that hovered over everything—and am even more unprepared for my mother's reaction to it all. She was cheerful and optimistic last night at dinner. Now her sadness has returned. She seems genuinely distressed by Munch's angst, anguish, and desolation. As we walk through the gallery, she sighs a lot and shakes her head. Whatever was distracting her earlier has returned with a vengeance.

I've got to find a way to get her away from all this doom and gloom. Fast.

"Change of plans," I tell her. I hurry her out of the museum and into a taxi. I tell the driver to take us to Troldhaugen, the Edvard Grieg Museum. Everything I've read about it makes it sound like a happy, cheerful place, and it is: a wonderful sunny yellow Victorian house on a magnificent piece of property, right on Lake Nordas. The place where the fabulous composer lived, loved, and wrote.

Walking around with the docent, I marvel at the water views from practically every room. There's a little cottage Grieg built right on the water's edge, just for composing. We walk down to it and look in one of the cottage windows. The place looks empty except for Grieg's original piano and a couch.

How wonderful it must have been to hunch over

the keys, strains of *Peer Gynt* songs floating through your head, then look out the window and watch the water roll by.

I've always loved water views. And I've always loved water. I was captain of my high school swim team and state champion in the 50- and 100-yard freestyle. Dr. Liz never came anywhere near a bake sale or class trip to *The Nutcracker,* but she never missed a swim meet. True, she initially encouraged me for the wrong reason ("Swimming is a great way to slim down"), but the more I got into it, the more seriously she began to take it.

Of course, there were also times she and I butted heads. *No surprise there.* My mother has strong opinions about everything, even things she knows little about. She used to sit in the stands with a stopwatch, a heat sheet, and a pencil. So did Lorraine Minerva, another swimmer's mother. But Lorraine only kept track of her daughter's splits. My mother kept track of everybody's, and took notes on my performance, which she graciously shared:

You had a slow start...

You went out too fast...

You didn't finish strong enough...

All this from a woman whose only previous relationship with water was to add it to her Johnny Walker Black.

Still, my mother was my biggest cheerleader. I was recruited by several Pac-12 and Southeastern

Conference schools, but I really wanted a Big 10. So when the scholarship came through at the University of Wisconsin–Madison, she was beyond thrilled.

"What are you thinking about?" she asks me now.

"All those times you came to my swim meets. Remember?"

She smiles. "Of course. I couldn't take my eyes off you. You really knew what you were doing back then."

Back then. On any other day, I might take that as a veiled slight that really means "Of course, *now* you seem to mess everything up." But not today.

"I was surprised when you got hooked on swimming," my mother says. "You were never much of a jock."

No, I wasn't. But *she* was. And because she was so good at tennis and golf and running, I never attempted any of those.

Over the years, I tried yoga, aerobics, kickboxing, jogging, even tango lessons to stay in shape. I still do some of those (not enough, Dr. Liz would say).

But none ever really grabbed me.

Swimming was different. It fit me. I loved the feeling of being in the water—smooth and sleek. Quiet. Enveloping. And I loved that everyone on the team had the same body issues I did. Finally, I didn't feel so alone. We treated the training table like an endless smorgasbord, then starved ourselves off-season.

I always felt confident in water. It took me years

(with the help of The Great Esther) to feel that way on land.

"Watching you compete was thrilling. I was so proud of you."

"Really?" I had no idea she felt that way.

"Of course."

I feel myself start to well up. Good thing she didn't mention it back then. It's hard to cry underwater.

"I loved having you there for moral support," I say.

Have I ever told her that before? I don't think so.

We walk to the shoreline of Grieg's lake and watch a few seagulls dive for fish as the sun begins to set. I feel calm and peaceful. I think it's the water. But it could just as well be thinking about Richard. Full disclosure— despite what I tell my mother, I can't stop the happily-ever-after fantasies. Fantasy One: Richard follows me all the way back to New York. He makes the rounds of law firms, lands a job at Cravath, Swaine & Moore, and we move in together. Fantasy Two: Richard convinces me to move to London. I make the rounds of advertising agencies, land a job at McCann Worldgroup, and we move in together.

When we last said goodbye, we made plans for him to meet my mother tonight. A simple dinner, just the three of us. Then after dinner he'll whisk me off to his hotel for what might be our last night together for a while. The only problem: I still haven't told my mother that Richard is here.

My phone buzzes. It's him.

Okay if I put off meeting Mum for a bit?

Maybe do dinner, just the two of us?

I don't ask him why. I think I'm sort of relieved. I'm feeling very close to my mother right now. It's been a lovely afternoon. Why ruin it? But this means now I have to do something I know I'm going to regret.

I'm going to have to lie to her.

CHAPTER 46

AKSEL HANSEN WAS ON the Norwegian Olympic swim team as a teenager. Soon after a stunning showing at the games, he was recruited by the University of Wisconsin–Madison. A freestyler and a heartthrob, Aksel was a slim handsome powerhouse—as fast with the ladies as he was in the pool. I might be the only woman on the swim team he didn't sleep with. We were just friends. After graduation, he moved back to Norway and married. Years later, when he and his wife divorced, he reached out for comfort—a long sad email—and we got back in touch, commiserating over our divorces.

I reached out to him when planning this trip, and since he lives near Bergen, we decided to meet up. I tell my mother I'm meeting Aksel for a drink, and she's fine with that.

Some of his friends might be joining us, I lied, covering my plans to meet up with Richard. I tell her not to wait up for me, that Aksel and his friends and I would probably all go out to dinner and then head to a club. She's okay with that plan, too.

The place Aksel picks is a dark, obscure hole-in-the-wall bar that only a local would know. It's been years since I've seen him. I barely recognize the paunchy, pudgy man waving to me. The classic biceps and triceps are still there. So is the sexy swagger. But his once-handsome face now shows the beginnings of jowly middle age. And his life has fared no better than his body. He's bounced around from career to career, he tells me. The little money he makes goes straight to child support.

Naturally, for a man who feels he peaked at eighteen, Aksel wants to talk about the old days. We throw around a lot of *whatever happened to*s, sharing information on various people we knew back then, some of whom have gone on to fame or fortune or neither or both. By the time we hug goodbye, I've got a slight wine buzz on.

Now it's time to see Richard.

We're meeting at a seafood restaurant on the prom-enade. Enhjørningen (the name means *Unicorn*) is in one of the old warehouses on the harbor that dates from the Middle Ages. Now meticulously restored, they're home to wonderful craft shops, art galleries, and restaurants.

Richard is waiting for me, his hair still wet from a shower. I kiss him on the cheek. He smells like pa-tchouli. Tonight, he's wearing a Wedgwood-blue shirt, a classic blue blazer, and Weejuns without socks. I love the look: half choirboy, half preppy. He takes my hand and we go inside.

The walls are painted a bright lime green, with vin-tage oil paintings everywhere. It's relaxing and elegant. Richard watches as I look around.

"I hope you like my choice," he says. "I was looking for someplace posh."

Posh. The perfect word.

"I love it," I say.

Our waiter, Einar, takes our drink order. I try their special martini: caraway-flavored aquavit, gin, and vermouth with a touch of orange bitters and a sliver of orange rind on the rim. It's delicious.

"So, you chickened out about meeting my mother," I say.

"Well, I don't know if I'd put it quite like that," he says. "It was more that, uh, it didn't seem, well...ap-propriate. What with the three of us dining, and then the two of us dashing off..."

I keep forgetting. He's *veddy veddy* British.

"Besides," he adds, "we only have this one day together."

Einar tells us about tonight's specials: smoked whale ham with lingonberry sauce and tarragon to start, then herb-fried anglerfish with morels. Sounds good to both of us.

"I do love some of these names," Richard says, as the waiter bows and departs. "Herb Fried Angler-fish. Doesn't that sound like a very upper-class British writer?"

"Yes," I say. "I wonder if Herb knows Rosemary Roasted Chicken."

"Brilliant," he says, laughing. "And I'm sure you've heard about the great female mathematician: Lois Carmen Denominator." Damn if this guy isn't as clever as he is charming, and as charming as he is handsome. And no, I do not tell him any of that.

We go on and on like this for a while, delighting each other with funny names—Ann Chovy, Chris P. Bacon, Norman Conquest—until our appetizers arrive. Then we compare our afternoons. Mine with the two Edvards, Munch and Grieg, sounds much more inter-esting than his days of answering phone calls, emails, and texts from the office.

"That's the problem with technology today," I say. "You can run but you can't hide."

"Exactly," he says.

Einar, our waiter, comes by to whisk away our whale plates and serve the anglerfish.

"I never had this before," I tell him.

"I'm not surprised," Einar says. "Anglerfish live in the darkest part of the ocean and have a dorsal fin that contains millions of light-producing bacteria. To attract a mate, that fin glows in the dark and pulses."

Richard smiles his adorable smile. I'm tempted to make a joke about how those fish could learn a lot about attraction from my tablemate. But I decide against it.

"Let me know if there's anything else you need," Einar says.

Richard puts his hand across the table to hold mine. "Thank you," he says, "but I've got everything I need right here." Einar smiles and leaves.

I'm probably blushing. Luckily for an emotional grab bag like me, I'm not tearing up. And, if I am, well, mercifully, the restaurant is dimly lit.

I cut off a piece of the anglerfish and take a bite. It's soft and chewy and reminds me a little of lobster. Every time I put down my knife, Richard takes my hand again. It's sweet, really. Every diet book I've ever read advises you to eat slowly. I can't think of a better way to do that.

Then it's time for dessert.

We have *lun rabarbrapai*, a fluffy rhubarb-and-vanilla pie with caramel ice cream. We order one slice to share. I'm so into this guy, I even find it exciting when our forks touch.

He's probably planning to bring me back to his hotel. But I have a better idea.

"Listen," I say, "would you be up for something really quirky?"

He puts down his fork and turns serious. "Um. That depends. Uh, exactly *how* kinky?"

I laugh. "I didn't say kinky. I said *quirky.*"

"Oh." He's smiling again. "Well...What did you have in mind?"

CHAPTER 47

SO INSTEAD OF HEADING to his room at the very chic, very glamorous Hotel Norge, I bring him back to my place. The minute he steps into the lobby and sees the dangling spidery iron chandeliers, he starts to laugh.

"Barmy!" he says. "Do they leave chocolates on your pillow at night...or just jack-o'-lanterns?"

"Wait'll you see the rest of it," I say. We duck into the pink/aqua/purple neon-lighted elevator. Richard looks around as the color lights rapidly change. He smiles. "I thought disco was dead."

We make our way to my pitch-black room. I turn on the lights—or, more precisely, the *light*. A single, dangling, postmodern overhead bulb that barely makes a difference. The room with its black walls and purple tiles is still gloomy and shadowy. But who cares?

"Good thing we had garlic on that fish," Richard says.

"Why?" I ask.

"This way, I can still find you in the dark."

We laugh and kiss and tumble into bed still dressed. Like teenagers, we're in too much of a hurry to waste time taking off our clothes. I'm feeling on top of the world tonight.

It's not until later on, lying in his arms, breathless and spent, that I start dreading tomorrow. Dr. Liz and I are flying north to what's literally the top of the world: the city of Alta. My mother and I will be looking at the northern lights while Richard flies back to London.

I try not to think about it. *A final goodbye?* I don't think I can bear it. But to my surprise and delight, Richard brings his face closer to mine and announces that he has "a perfectly lovely Plan B."

"Okay. Tell me fast before my heart breaks," I say.

"After Alta, you head back to Oslo for your flight to America, right?"

"After we visit some relatives. Yes."

"If you let me know what day you'll be back in Oslo, I'll arrange to be back there, too."

"In Oslo? Really?"

"Oslo. Really. What do you say to that?"

It's so dark, I'm not sure he can see me smiling.

CHAPTER 48

SUDDENLY IT'S TOMORROW. MEETING up again in Oslo seems a million light-years away. I'm not ready to let him go. How can I possibly say goodbye?

I have another idea. Not quirky this time. Just devious.

"Are you a breakfast person?" I ask him after we shower and dress.

"Sure. Why?"

"I hear they have a great breakfast here. Why don't you join us?"

He hesitates. I keep talking. "The buffet here is supposed to be incredible: gravlax, oatmeal, pastries, fruit smoothies, pastrami, different kinds of breads and berries, all kinds of fish spreads and . . ."

He's shaking his head. "It's not the food I'm concerned about," he says. "It's the 'us' part."

"Here's my plan. We'll make believe we don't know each other. I'll sit with my mother. You'll be at a nearby table, checking her out."

This guy brings out the playful side of me. Even better, I know he feels the same.

"You're on," he says. Then we pause for a moment. He moves toward me, and we share a long, deep kiss. As we kiss, I enter a beautiful world of hazy thought. What I'm thinking is: *I guess I lied to my mother about this, too. Maybe I am in love with him.*

We move apart, and he says, "All good things must etcetera."

We take the elevator downstairs.

When we get down to the lobby, I find my mother already at a table. I join her while Richard heads to the *koldtbord* buffet and gets on the line. At one point I see him look at me, then at my mother, then at me again. I can't wait to hear what he thinks. I keep trying to catch his eye. Of course, eagle-eyed Dr. Liz notices.

"Looking for someone?" she asks. *Busted!*

"I invited Aksel to join us for breakfast," I lie. "So I'm checking to see if he's here."

To make my lie seem truthful, I embellish it. I tell her where Aksel and his friends and I went last night, what kind of music we danced to, what we ate. I'm on a roll. But my mother seems to have lapsed into one of her quiet introspective moods and doesn't register any of it.

After some yogurt, fresh strawberries, and a few cups of coffee, I add another lie: "I need to go back to my room to finish packing."

My mother makes a face. Our flight isn't until early evening, and she wanted to get in some shopping before we left.

We agree to meet on the wharf after I check out. She leaves. I wait until she's safely out of sight before I walk over to Richard, sitting alone at a corner table. I look around to make sure my mother hasn't sneaked back. She hasn't.

"So what do you think?" I ask him.

"Handsome woman, your mum," he says. "Makes quite an impression. Must say, a tad dishier than I might have thought."

"Dishier?"

"Oh. Sorry. More *attractive*. Though a wee bit stern."

"Exactly. Perfect description. You got her."

"I can see the two of you clashing. Well," he says, looking at his watch. "It's barely ten. Now what?" He knows checkout time is noon.

"I still have some packing to do. Actually, more folding than packing."

"Folding! My good woman, I'll have you know, I am the folding champion of East London!" he says, with a twinkle in his eye. "In fact, as a boy scout, I once earned an activity badge in folding." The twinkling doesn't stop but now he's added a smile.

He puts his arm around me and we head back upstairs.

CHAPTER 49

MY MOTHER AND I are all checked in at the Bergen Airport. It's official: she has now spent more on oversize baggage fees than on plane tickets.

We watch one of her two giant suitcases ride the conveyor belt to the fuselage, her other stored back at the hotel with the concierge. Then we head to the SAS Café Lounge to await our flight. I still haven't told her that Richard is here in Bergen, or that he spent the night (and most of the morning) with me at our hotel. His own flight to London isn't till later. Still, I look around to check if he's here. There's no sign of him. I'm sort of relieved.

I see a smattering of tourists, and a few well-behaved children. Most of the people here seem to be Scandinavian. About half the men and women are carrying briefcases and fancy leather overnight bags.

One man in particular catches my eye: he's in his

late sixties with wavy hair the color of straw. It's reced-
ing quite a bit in the front. He's deeply engaged in a
newspaper and occasionally frowning at whatever he's
reading. He's wearing a navy suit and a white button-
down shirt, no tie.

I can't stop looking at him.

The guy is a dead ringer for my late father.

I nudge my mother. As usual, she has her head
buried in a professional journal. This one is filled with
various color photos of a uterus.

"Check out that guy," I say, nodding my head in his
direction. She looks at him. Then she smiles.

"Doesn't he remind you of . . . ?"

"Your father. Yes." We watch the man for a few
moments, trying not to stare. He stands up and takes
off his suit jacket, then folds it neatly and puts it on the
seat next to him.

"Your father did that, too," she says. "He hated when
his suits were wrinkled."

We're both silent for a moment feeling a little . . . something. Wistful? Sad? Maybe both. We have a while until
our flight. It's as good a moment as any to ask some
things I've always wanted to ask.

"Tell me something about my father," I say. "Something I don't know."

The question takes her by surprise.

She closes her magazine. "Like what?" She is looking
at me with uncharacteristic concern.

"What it was like for you? What's the secret of your long, happy marriage?"

She pauses. "You think our marriage was happy?" she asks.

I look at her. *Is she kidding?* That's like asking if I think the sky is blue.

"Well," she says. "Your father adored me." Exactly. "The sun rose and set on me. I don't know why he felt that way. I am not... well, I'm not a giving, generous person by nature. *He* was the generous one."

"You were generous," I say, not quite sure why I'm leaping to her defense. "You always gave me..."

"I mean generous of *spirit*. He always teased me that when it came to love, I was... stingy."

Good thing we don't have to board for another hour. I need some time to process all this.

"I was always so busy with medical school and interning and the hours I kept and staying on top of all my patients," she says. "Back then a woman had to work so much harder than men, just to stay in place."

It's not that different now, I think. But I don't want to interrupt her.

"So, were we happy? I guess love is really a skill. Like any skill, you have to practice to get really good at it. And I never had much time to practice."

(NOTE TO SELF: Try to remember all this, the next time you have a session with Esther.)

"Even with you," she says. "You were the most

adorable baby. Everybody who saw you said so. Big smiles for everyone who walked into the room, who poked their head in the carriage. But I never..."

She takes a deep breath. There is a long pause. "This will sound much worse than I mean it: I never felt anything for you. Not how a mother is supposed to feel."

Wait. What?

Never?

"I was always more interested in the rational, factual side of things," she says.

"A disease, a symptom. I guess that's what made me a great physician...and a not-so-great mother."

It's true. But hearing her say this breaks my heart.

"I'm being honest," she says. "As a child, you were perfect, and I...wasn't."

She turns away suddenly, afraid to look at me. Does she think I'm going to be angry at her for what she's just said? Hardly. I'm feeling a little anger, sure. But also compassion, curiosity, and relief. *So it wasn't just my imagination,* I think. She *was* cold to me. The sadness I feel is tempered by the relief of knowing I wasn't just making things up.

Forget a therapy session: I'm tempted to text Esther right now.

"Did you love Dad?" I ask.

There is a long pause. A very looooooong pause.

"Your father was a very decent, loving man," she says. "It was hard not to care deeply about him."

My poor father. He spent most of his life trying to make her happy. I wonder if he knew how little all that effort paid off.

"Did Dad know about your mystery man?" I ask.

"We never discussed it," she says. I'm glad about that. I was devastated when Andrew told me he preferred someone else. My father deserved better than that.

They are making an announcement about our flight. We both stop to listen. The timing couldn't be worse. It draws our conversation to an immediate close. There's a lot more to be said, but my mother goes back to her glossy magazine with the uterine pictures, back to the world she's most comfortable in, a world where she can keep her secrets safe.

All around us, people are grabbing their bags and heading to the gate. But my mother is in no hurry. She does not believe in fighting for overhead space. Besides, all her luggage is checked.

As always, she will be the last to board.

CHAPTER 50

THIS IS THE COLDEST I have ever been.

Alta is just south of the Arctic Circle. It's only October, yet there's already a foot of snow on the ground. We slip and slide our way across the few feet from where the taxi lets us off to the entrance to our hotel.

Did I say hotel? Make that "rustic lodge"—a primitive building in the middle of nowhere. It has wooden beams, the original eighteenth-century wood floors, a communal table for meals...and not enough heat. Leisel and Hans, the owners, have graciously provided extra blankets, but it makes little difference. Our rooms are freezing.

I know what my mother is about to ask. I decide to head her off. "There *are* no luxury hotels up here," I say.

No one comes to Alta for the creature comforts. You come for the lights, the weather, or the dogs. Alta is the starting point for the annual Finnmarksløpet, the longest sled dog race in Europe. Virtually everyone in Alta either owns, raises, or races huskies.

She says nothing.

After a simple late-night dinner (beer, hot fish soup, fresh-from-the-oven bread), we go upstairs and decide to sleep in our clothes. We set our alarms to wake us up in time for breakfast. We didn't need to—at daybreak, we hear barking. We look out the window. There are doghouses scattered all across the property, with hungry dogs chained to all of them.

Several unchained huskies are wandering around the grounds. They begin jumping up and slobbering on the picture window near where my mother and I are having breakfast. I hold my hand on the inside of the glass and they start to lick it.

"That's so sweet," I say.

"Really? I think it's disgusting."

Since "disgusting" trumps "sweet," we hurry through our meal (*havregrøt,* an oat cereal with cinnamon, and a *bolle,* a sweet bread roll) and head back upstairs for our coats.

My mother unpacks her winter gear: a Canada Goose down coat and hood, sealskin Topaz snow boots, woolen socks (two pairs), a woolen hat, fur-lined gloves, hand-warmers, foot-warmers, two extra cashmere sweaters for her, two for me, and a scarf. It takes a while to put all our layers on.

Our young guide is already downstairs waiting for us. Nils has the robust healthy look of someone used to the cold. His cheeks are rosy. He's wearing gloves, but no hat. Worse, his dirty-blond hair has bits of ice in it, as if he just stepped out of the shower and decided to let it air-dry.

My mother frowns. "You realize your hair won't be dry until spring," she says to him in English.

I can't believe how rude she is. But Nils only laughs.

"Not to worry," he says to me as he shakes our multi-gloved hands. "In Alta, we have a saying. *Du kan alltid si det til en turist når de skjelver.* You can always tell a tourist by the way they shiver."

Nils tells us he's a student here. Not surprisingly, he graduated with a degree in outdoor Arctic recreation, and is now going for a master's in sports science.

There's not a lot to see in Alta. But since the sun sets at three in the afternoon, that won't be a problem. Our first stop is the Alta Museum's World Heritage Rock Art Centre, where we join a small group of people on a tour of Alta's claim to fame: UNESCO-protected rock carvings. But the tour is only of the digital archives.

"Where are the actual carvings?" my mother asks. The docent points to the window and shrugs. "Out there," she says. "But most of year, they're covered with snow."

Our next stop: several glass cases filled with weapons and instruments made of brass, leather, and wood. My mother rolls her eyes. "Didn't we already see this at the Viking Ship Museum?" she asks. She's right.

But then comes a surprise: a visual time-lapse show of 365 photos taken at 365 successive noons in Svalbard, a remote area halfway between here and the North Pole. In fifteen minutes, I get to experience a year in the Land of the Midnight Sun, and it's totally thrilling.

At least *I* think so. My mother disagrees. I assume she's just being difficult. But then I realize: *she's already lived it.*

Like all good tours, this one ends with a visit to the gift shop. It's filled with scarves, paperweights, tote bags with the museum's logo—nothing that strikes my mother's fancy. As I check out the key chains, she is clearly bored and getting antsy.

"Tell me again why we came to Alta?" she says.

She knows why: because I've always wanted to see the northern lights. Her parents had taken her on family vacations to see them, twice, when she was a child. Both nights were cloudy, and she was disappointed. She warns me I will be, too. But I don't care. It's the one thing I've insisted on, in exchange for giving up two weeks of my vacation time for her benefit.

I walk away from her, rather than say something I know I'll regret.

Nils suggests a number of other activities: the Tirpitz War Museum, a hike, a sleigh ride. We pass on all but say yes to the Northern Lights Cathedral. It turns out to be a stunning modern building with a spiral on top. It's not just a church, but also a cultural center. We're too early for the piano concerts, and too late for services. But right next door to the cathedral is a huge aquatic center with a 25-meter training pool. Who knew?

"Too bad you didn't bring a bathing suit," my mother says. Yes, that might have been nice and reminiscent of old times. But get into a bathing suit? I'd be the first to admit that I'm out of shape.

No, wait. I'd be the second. My mother would beat me to it.

Now what? Our official northern lights tour doesn't start for several hours. So we decide to take the scenic route back to the lodge. We pass a hill filled with a herd of thirty reindeer, many with jingling bells around their neck. It's the perfect Alta photo op, so Nils stops and we get out of the car. But almost all of them have their backs to us: not the greatest view. My mother walks over to the chain-link fence surrounding them and taps it. Then she makes a few odd sounds. Sure enough, a few of the reindeer turn around to look at her. Then they come closer to where she's standing. I get some great photos of a few of them desperately trying to give her a kiss through the links.

Amazing. In addition to all her other credentials, my mother is also a reindeer whisperer. Something new to add to her CV.

Behind these magnificent animals are hills covered

with frozen icicles, and trees where the snow has formed thousands of tiny snowflakes. I take lots of exquisite panoramic shots. I feel like I'm standing in the middle of a Christmas card.

It's getting late in the afternoon. As we head up the coast, we watch the rich blue colors of water and sky slowly turn into the golds and oranges of a late-afternoon sunset. It is totally quiet, totally peaceful. Even Dr. Liz is unusually silent as we take in the breathtaking views. This might be the closest to a Zen moment that she and I have ever shared.

Back at the lodge, my mother heads upstairs and I wander around the grounds a bit. Across from the entrance, what I thought was a larger-than-life doghouse turns out to be a shed that sells handmade mittens and scarves. I walk in and find I am all alone; no customers, no salesperson. All the items have price tags. Customers are on the honor system. I smile to myself, wondering how long a self-service shop like this would last in New York.

Around the back there is a wonderful old-fashioned cheese store that probably started life as a log cabin. All the shelves and walls are paneled in beautiful old wood, with signs that say SURDEIG and NOKKELOST and TORJULVÅGEN KRAFTKAR. I think they're cheeses. They could be breads. The shelves are empty. I guess it's off-season.

I need to check in with my office. I head back to my

room and get under the covers to read my emails. And of course, I want to text Richard. It takes me a while to think of what to say. "Miss you already"? That sounds a little...pushy? Needy? Neither one feels right. I don't want him to think I'm pining away for him, although I am. I want him to think of me as the strong, charming woman he's smitten with, someone without a lot of emotional baggage.

So I opt for something that will make him laugh:

Having wonderful time. Wish you were *her*.

CHAPTER 51

THE NORTHERN LIGHTS REMIND me a lot of my mother.

They're persnickety. They're used to having their own way. And they don't really care what other people want.

We're standing outside a huge black van in the darkest, blackest place I've ever been. Everyone in our little group (Fiona and Sean from Ireland, Walter Call-Me-Wally from Germany, Desi and Anna from England) is wearing a full-body windbreaker that looks like a shiny yellow hazmat suit, courtesy of our tour company. We're also given goggles and special hats.

The thermometer measures zero degrees Celsius. The wind whips across my face. *Hard to believe it's only October.*

"What must it be like here in winter?" I ask.

Sara, our guide, answers me very seriously. "In

winter, it is *really* cold." She's one of the trifecta people; she came here for the lights, the weather, *and* the dogs. During the day, when she's not giving tours, she teaches snowboarding and trains huskies. And when she's not doing any of those, she's a professional knitter. She pulls out her cell phone to show us some of her designs.

We look up at the sky and wait. And wait. And wait. That's what seeing the northern lights entails: you wait, and you freeze. My mother, who's used to waiting for hours until a baby is ready to be born, has no problem waiting. I think she's looking forward to the moment she can turn to me and say "*I told you so.*" Meanwhile, she and the others get into a rousing discussion of places they've been, things they've seen, foods they've eaten. It always amazes me how chatty Dr. Liz can be when she decides to turn on the charm.

An hour passes. Fiona, Anna, and I have gotten in and out of the van several times, trying to keep warm. At one point Sara knocks on the window and offers us hot chocolate. We all take a cup. It's delicious.

"Who wants more?" Sara asks. I do. But I don't ask. Because even in the dark, I can see my mother giving me The Look.

The Look. Something she's been doing since I was a small child. Even without words, her face can convey a million things—all of them disapproving:

Don't do that.

Leave that alone.

You've had enough.

You're doing it all wrong.

It's always a variation of the same thing: *"No daughter of mine should do/say/wear/eat something like that."*

Three hours later as we're still staring up at the sky, some vague whitish clouds slowly drift into view. *Is that all there is?* The temperature is dropping. We're all growing a little impatient, stamping our feet to keep warm. I hate to admit: my mother may have been right. Sara has been on her cell phone for a while, calling other northern lights chasers around Norway to share their viewing conditions and hear the latest aurora forecast predictions.

Then, suddenly, things begin to change.

Sara is the one who spots it first, of course. It's a kind of radar she's developed, after years of doing this. "Look," she says, pointing off to the left of the white haze. We see a teeny bit of green, the color of lime Jell-O. Then more green. Then a flurry of green that floats across the sky, picking up a tiny bit of blue along the way.

The lights move gradually, as slow as a cloud, but the hues are vivid and beautiful. We wait and watch. The colors widen as they move, forming gorgeous Rorschach patterns. A green duck, followed by a chunk of violet. Then a bit of bronze and gold chasing all of it, trying to keep up. All against the dusty background made up of a trillion tiny pinpoint stars.

Meanwhile, Sara starts setting up a 35mm camera and tripod. We all queue up to have our pictures taken with the northern lights backdrop. It looks like we're standing in front of a dreamy spectrum of fairy dust, swirled with color, silently swooshing across the sky.

Soon it's time to pile into the van and head back. My mother is in the front this time. I am diagonally behind her. At one point, she turns around. I decide to give her my own version of The Look. A somewhat sarcastic smirk that can only mean one thing:

See? I told you so.

CHAPTER 52

I'VE CROSSED THE NORTHERN lights off my bucket list. We've seen pretty much everything Alta has to offer. So next morning as we're checking out, my mother surprises me when she says, "Maybe we should spend a few extra days here."

Then it sinks in: *she's trying to delay our trip to her relatives.* I decide to play dumb.

"What would we do here?" I ask.

"We can...relax?" she says. It's not a word she says very often. It sticks in her throat.

"Relax how?" I ask. I stump her on this one. There are no spas, no shops worth visiting, and not enough time for even a minor cosmetic procedure.

We stick to our plans and return to Oslo. When we land, I rent a car. I assume I'll be driving directly to Kongsvinger, her hometown, just over an hour to the northeast. But no. Another delay tactic: my mother wants to head into the city first so she can stop at our hotel and reconfirm our return reservation.

"We can do that online," I tell her.

"I want to do it in person," she says.

"That's a waste of time. We can do it online."

"I . . . want . . . to . . . do . . . it . . . in . . . person."

So we do.

At the hotel, my mother decides to retrieve the suitcase she had left with the concierge. *Seriously?* Kongsvinger is a small town of farms and tiny villages. How many changes of clothing does she think she'll need for two days?

I don't argue with her. But as the doorman loads her bag into the trunk, I can't resist a small dig. "It's probably better to have everything," I say. "Just in case you decide to move back."

At this point in our journey, we're both weary and crabby and—should I say it?—a little tired of each other. Paris had lots of diversions. Norway has been a bit of a strain. For every lighthearted moment, there's been one when I wanted to throw her under a fast-moving sled. It's like what Stephen Sondheim once wrote:

Good things get better, bad get worse.

Wait—I think I meant that in reverse.

Of course, Sondheim was talking about marriage. But the sentiment holds true for the two of us.

My mother's sister, Jeannie, has been emailing how excited she is, about the luncheon she's planning, about the people she's invited. We'll be meeting her children, friends, and neighbors that remember dear Lissa. (*Lissa?*) She's even dug up an old box of family photos.

As we get closer to my aunt's home, my mother stares out the window. I'm expecting her to point out some of the places she remembers—*There's where my best friend lived! There's my old school! There's where I had my first kiss!*—but she stays completely silent.

"Here's something that might cheer you up," I say. "I've booked us into a castle. The Kongsvinger Castle."

"It's *not* a castle," she snaps. "It's a hotel built inside the Kongsvinger Fortress."

Oh.

"If you *really* wanted to do something nice for me, you should have booked us into the Rømskog Spa & Resort."

Snap.

That's not the engine belt inside the car. It's something inside of *me*. I put on my hazards, pull over to the side of the road, and turn off the engine.

"Something wrong?" my mother asks.

"*Wrong?*" I'm trying not to laugh. "Well, I guess you could say that. See, I thought I was doing a nice thing, planning this surprise reunion. But you've done everything in your power to make me feel bad about it, and guilty, and like a worthless piece of—"

"I'm sorry," she says. It falls flat.

"No. *I'm* sorry. Sorry I ever agreed to take you on

this trip. Sorry I thought we'd really learn to like each other. Sorry I had the crazy thought that at some point you'd turn to me and say, 'What a great idea this was. What a great daughter you are.'"

"Laurie, I—"

"I'm...not...finished!" I yell. We're both shocked at my tone. "Most people—*normal* people—enjoy a family reunion. But nothing pleases you. Once again, I did the wrong thing. You don't want to see your relatives? Fine. I don't want to take you anywhere you don't want to go."

"I didn't say—"

"I'll make up a story. I'll say we had to fly back to New York for some, I don't know, work emergency? A crisis at my office or some damn thing."

I get out and lean against the rental as other cars zip by. I'm dying for a Klonopin, a Xanax, a drink, maybe even a cigarette—even though I never smoked. Anything to calm me down. Instead, I take a few deep breaths. I keep imagining the look on Esther's face when I tell her what my mother said: "If you *really* wanted to do something nice for me..."

After a while I get back in the car and turn the engine back on. I don't look at her.

I hear her say "I'm sorry" again. This time it sounds like she means it.

At this point, I no longer care.

We pull up to the hotel, and it turns out she's right:

The Castle is not really a castle. It's a hotel built inside the walls of a perfectly restored historic fortress. Still, it's a lovely combination of elegance and old-world hospitality, with magnificent views.

The porter seems surprised by all our luggage. "Just the two of you?" he asks.

"Yes," I say. He probably thinks we're staying for months.

He puts our bags on his trolley and takes them up to our rooms as my mother and I get back in the car. The crisis point has passed. That argument took a lot out of me. I turn on the GPS, and we drive in silence. I don't have the energy to talk. I feel spent. No, not spent.

Squandered.

CHAPTER 53

JEANNIE'S HOUSE IS ONE of eight small white wood two-story houses on the block. It looks a little whiter than the others, as if it was recently painted. For us, I wonder? The house has wooden shutters the color of walnuts, a gray slate roof, and a small patch of grass in front.

Several cars are parked in front of the place. I park behind them. Then we ring the bell. We hear a lot of commotion coming from inside.

My mother's sister opens the door. You'd think we were the people from Publishers Clearing House delivering a surprise million-dollar check. Jeannie screams. Her eyes fill with tears. "They're here!" she cries out. *"Velkommen!"*

She leans over and hugs my mother. It's quite touching. I find myself tearing up. Then my aunt takes a step backward and looks at her sister for the first time in almost fifty years.

"Hello, Jeannie," my mother says.

Jeannie cries some more and hugs her again.

Several people pop up behind her: a pretty young woman in her thirties, a taller woman holding a baby, five small children, a few men, some other people, and an elderly woman leaning on a cane. All of them crowd around us and take turns hugging my mother. It's like the receiving line at a wedding, and Dr. Liz is the bride.

Did I say bride? It's more like guest of honor. Turns out, my mother is a local celebrity around here. They've been following her career online all these years. I'm still angry at her, but I get it: the woman who left their tiny off-the-map town for college and medical school in America, then traveled around the world teaching thousands of women about safe pregnancies and good reproductive health. If she wasn't my mother, I'd be impressed too.

Jeannie puts her arm around her sister and leads her to the couch. The others grab chairs and surround her. In quick succession we're introduced to Jeannie's two daughters, Anne Marie and Emma Matilda, and everyone else. I must confess, as an only child, there is something touching about meeting so many new relatives. Especially since they all seem so happy to meet me.

They have a million questions for both of us, but mostly for my mother. They speak in English, for my benefit, but slip into Norwegian now and then when they get excited. *What's it like, being a woman doctor? How does it feel to be back? What can you tell us about the world you've seen?*

My mother takes a sip of the aquavit they've handed her and begins the lecture I've heard many times before. "The thing you have to realize," she says, "is how lucky we all are to be living in a country like this or America, where health care is available." She starts to talk about Third World countries and superstitions about child-bearing. Dr. Liz is charming, caring, and professional. She always is, around groups like this. And they always adore her. She's like a Pied Piper for fertile women.

Meanwhile, I've got a few questions of my own. "What was my mother like as a child?" I ask Jeannie.

"The smartest girl in the class," she says without skipping a beat.

"Oh, I don't know if that's true," my mother says, uncharacteristically modest.

"Mabel Nelson was always..."

"No!" Jeannie is shaking her head furiously. "Mabel Nelson could never compete with you. Well, except for that spelling competition." Jeannie and my mother look at each other and crack up.

"What happened there?" I ask.

"Every Friday in class, we had a spelling bee. It was a way for us to practice our English. Your mother usually won. She had an unbroken record. Then one Friday, she tripped up on the word *carnivore*. She thought they said *carnival*."

"I was recovering from a bad cold," my mother says. "My ears were still clogged."

But Jeannie still isn't buying that, even after all these years. "She was always very competitive," Jeannie tells me. "Hated to lose. I bet she's still that way. Am I right?"

She pokes my mother affectionately. I wait to see if Dr. Liz is going to be annoyed, irritated, or pissed off.

To my surprise, she giggles.

CHAPTER 54

I'M ON MY SECOND Ringnes, the locally brewed beer, when my cousins start putting out the buffet. And what a spread it is: brown *lapskaus* (pork, potato, and vegetable stew); *sodd* (mutton and meatballs); reindeer steaks; various fish dishes; salads, fruits, and pastries. They insist that my mother and I go first in line. To my surprise, she scoops up some of everything.

"Are these Vesteraalens?" my mother asks as she points to a platter of white ovals that look like fish balls. Jeannie nods yes.

"I used to love these as a little girl," she tells me.

"What are Vesteraalens?" I ask.

"It's a brand name," Jeannie says. "Like your Chef Boyardee."

"I never told Laurie about Mama's awful cooking," my mother confides to the crowd. "You know, in

America, the big thing now is farm-to-table. But when I grew up, it was cans-to-plate."

"Mama hated to cook," Jeannie tells them. "She felt eating was something you had to get through."

"Yes," my mother says. "Like sex."

We all burst out laughing. When did my mother become such a comedian?

We take our plates and settle back in our chairs. I watch as Jeannie and my mother chat quietly one-on-one. Jeannie is everything my mother isn't: gray-haired, heavyset, warm and outgoing. It's clear how glad she is to have her big sister there, glad to meet me, glad we showed up and put the old family rift behind us. Her eyes are big and blue like my mother's. But unlike my mother, her face is quite wrinkled. It's clear that they're all laugh lines. She's always smiling.

It's hard to believe these two sisters haven't talked in fifty years. "I am so sorry I was never able to meet Martin," Jeannie says at one point. She touches my mother's arm.

"Yes," my mother says. "He was a real family man. He would have enjoyed this."

Then Jeannie takes out a box of old photos. But as they wade through them, the talk suddenly segues to sad updates of all the people they have lost. A grim litany of tumors, strokes, accidents, suicides, disease, dementia. So many people, gone way too soon.

The tone of this conversation is doing no one any good, so I decide to change it.

"Where did the name Lissa come from?" I ask.

"Your mother's dumb baby sister," Jeannie says, laughing. "I couldn't say *Elizabeth*. All I could manage was *Lissa*. So she was Lissa from then on."

It is such a pleasant afternoon, full of people and food and memories. I can't understand my mother's reluctance to come here.

And then the front door opens.

CHAPTER 55

A GOOD-LOOKING MAN walks in. Late sixties, well over six feet, and definitely the outdoorsy type, with a full head of white hair. This must be Jeannie's husband, Tore Hamre, the farmer. He's wearing a plaid flannel shirt, jeans, and boots. He looks like the Marlboro man. Or maybe a lumberjack, someone used to lifting heavy objects.

Tore looks around the room until he finds what he's looking for. Or should I say *who.*

He smiles as he walks over to my mother.

"Lissa," he says, taking her hand and cupping it in both of his. "You haven't changed a bit."

Okay. It's a cliché. But a very gracious one. And my mother reacts graciously.

"That's very kind of you to say," she says.

Then he leans in and kisses her on both cheeks. Very

European. He is still holding her hand with both of his and looking at her.

"You must be Laurenne," he says, turning to me. "Well, welcome to our family! No. To *your* family." He gives me a hug. He cuts such a commanding figure, I expect him to have a booming voice, a crushing hug. But he doesn't.

"I hope they have been treating you right," he says, gesturing to the group.

"Most definitely," I say.

Tore kisses his wife hello and grabs a dinner plate, fills it high, and then reaches for a Hansa beer. The rest of us have peeled off into small groups of twos and threes. I'm sitting next to my cousin Anne Marie, one of Jeannie's daughters.

"My mother was so excited to get your email," Anne Marie says. "She was so looking forward to today."

"My mother was, too," I lie. I look over at my mother. She's chatting with Emma and bouncing Emma's baby on her lap. She seems to be having a good time, so I don't feel too guilty about the untruth.

"What do you do in New York?" Anne Marie asks. I give her a quick précis of Advertising 101 (even more condensed than the one I gave Richard). She says what everybody does: "That sounds exciting." So I say what I always do: "It is... sometimes."

Suddenly Tore stands up with his beer in hand. "We must toast!" he says. He holds the bottle up and begins to speak. "To all the years and all the miles between us," he says, looking at my mother. "May they be long forgotten, now that you're here."

I can see Aunt Jeannie begin to tear up. My mother says nothing, but nods as she bites her lower lip.

"*Skol!*" everybody says, raising a glass or a fork or whatever's handy. There is a murmur of congratulations. Then Tore turns to me.

"And to Laurenne," he says, "who made it all happen." *How did he know that?* I hear more *skols*, a few more cheers, and a "yay" or two. I look around; everyone is looking at me and smiling.

Maybe it's the beers, but I'm feeling nostalgic. I look over at my mother again. Emma has left to put the baby down for a nap, so my mother has moved over to make room on the couch for Tore. The two of them are talking quietly, their heads together.

Then Jeannie comes out of the kitchen, carrying a huge *bløtkake:* a traditional Norwegian birthday cake, they tell me. It's filled with pudding and peaches, topped with whipped cream and strawberries. But instead of *Happy Birthday,* the top says *Welcome Home.*

There are five candles on it. "One for every ten years you've been away," Anne Marie says.

They ask my mother to make a wish, and she does, silently. Then she blows out the candles. Everyone applauds, and we take turns posing for pictures, with my mother smiling at the center of each one.

Once the coffee and cake are finished, the party starts to wind down. A few more memories, a little more aquavit. My mother is still talking to Tore. At one point, she puts her hand on his shoulder. Very gently, he touches her hand with his.

Soon Dr. Liz stands up and heads over to me. "We should get going," she says. "It's been a long day." And it has. The trip to the Alta airport, the flight, our fight, seeing all these people for the first time in years. It has been physically and emotionally draining. But well worth it.

We start to say our goodbyes. "So soon?" Jeannie asks. "But you'll be back tomorrow, right? So many of the people in town want a chance to see you."

I'm about to say yes when my mother interrupts. "Wish we could," she says. "But we're heading back to America tomorrow."

We are?

Jeannie seems crushed.

"But we'll be back someday," my mother says.

"Oh you must," Jeannie says, "now that you see how much you've been missed."

The goodbye hugs take even longer than the hello ones did. After embracing everyone in the room, some twice, we make our way to the car. Everyone stands at the door waving goodbye as we pull away.

Despite my mother's reluctance to return tomorrow,

I'm feeling really good about my reunion idea, relieved that it worked out.

"That wasn't so terrible, was it?" I ask.

I look over at my mother. She's staring straight ahead. She says nothing for several miles.

Then, suddenly, she bursts into tears.

CHAPTER 56

I'VE NEVER SEEN HER like this.

Once again, we pull off to the shoulder of the road. But this time it's because my mother is hysterical. She didn't cry this hard when my father died, or when her best friend, Doris, died, or ever. I root around in my purse till I find a small pack of tissues. I give them to her. I'm actually too stunned to speak. There's nothing I can do but sit and wonder what this is all about.

She seemed to be so happy around her nieces, the friends and neighbors, and her sister and brother-in-law, Jeannie and Tore.

Suddenly it all falls into place.

But I can't ask her. At least not until she settles down a bit. After a while the tears turn into quiet sobs. She looks like hell. Her face is red and blotchy; her makeup is a mess. Even her lipstick, so carefully refreshed right before we left, is now smeared all over the tissues, all over her teeth. And all I can do is wait.

Finally, she takes a deep breath. It's my turn to speak. Do I dare?

"It was Tore, wasn't it?" I ask.

A pause. She looks at me. I think she's going to start crying again. "Yes," she says. It is the softest, quietest *yes* I ever heard.

There are so many questions roiling around in my brain, I don't know where to begin. But this dusty side of the road is neither the time nor the place.

"Is there anything I can do to . . . ?"

She shakes her head. Nothing will cheer her up, she says. Well, almost nothing. She opens her purse and takes out a chocolate bar the size of my arm. Freia Selskapssjokolade, the label says. *Et lite stykke Norge*. A little piece of Norway.

"Where did you get that?" I ask.

"From Nils," she says. "When you were poking around the keychain rack in the museum, Nils asked what I missed most, living in America. I mentioned Freia's. He dropped it off for me last night, while we were watching the northern lights."

"Sounds like you have a brand-new admirer," I say. For a split second I don't know if she's going to laugh or cry. She doesn't know, either. Then she starts to smile.

There are a million things I want to ask her. But for now, she breaks off a hunk of the chocolate for both of us.

One broken heart. One chocolate bar. Works every time.

CHAPTER 57

MY MOTHER WANTS OUT of Kongsvinger as quickly as possible. We confirm we can get into our Oslo hotel tonight. Then we check out of The Castle and head back.

As I drive, my mother tells me the whole story.

"I met Tore when we were children," she says. "We were seven, maybe younger. Right away we became best friends. He used to tell goofy jokes that made me laugh. From the very beginning, we were inseparable. I adored him."

She's quiet for a moment, smiling. I'm sure she's thinking about the old days.

She continues. "And then at some point—puberty, I suppose—our feelings took a deeper dive."

She sighs. "Everybody knew we were a two-some, but that didn't stop other girls. They flocked to him, threw themselves at him all through high school."

"Because he was good-looking?" I ask.

"Yes, and because he was a star player on our soccer team. Girls were always knitting him caps, scarves, gloves, and tossing flowers at him during the game. But if I was in the stands, well, he always made it a point to blow me a kiss."

"Sweet," I say. Actually, it sounds like a corny rom-com moment to me. But I don't think she needs to hear that.

"Tore was a great guy but not a great student, especially in math. So I tutored him. His friends teased him nonstop. 'You're only with her because you want to graduate,' they'd say. He laughed it off. We both did. But the fact is, he was basically a tall handsome jock, and I was..."

"The smartest girl in the class?" I ask. That's what Jeannie had called her.

"Well, yes," she says with uncharacteristic shyness. "When my friends were experimenting with lipstick and nail polish, I was experimenting with static electricity and cloud dough."

Cloud dough?

She sees my confusion. "It's something you make with flour and oil, instead of water. So it has a different viscosity."

"Oh," I say. I have no idea what she's talking about.

"I guess even then I was a nerd," she says, laughing.

It's good to hear her laugh again. "So there we were: the farm boy and the nerd. Then, when I was seventeen—"

All of a sudden my GPS interrupts. Damn it. *"In 500 meters, take the E-16 exit toward Lillestrøm."* I gotta hear how this ends. But to my mother's credit, she doesn't miss a beat.

"I began to volunteer at our local hospital. At first I was just wheeling the book cart around and handing out meal trays. But then I was assigned to the emergency room. That's what opened my eyes to the real world. Car crash victims with limbs hanging off. Colicky babies burned by angry parents. Women who were victims of domestic abuse. I was just a teenager, but I wanted desperately to help them all."

"Did Tore know that?"

"Yes. He said it was one of the things he loved about me. That I cared so much."

She's quiet for a moment. "I guess, if I had paid attention, I would have realized that he and I were never going to end the way I thought it would."

"What makes you say that?"

"For one thing, we never had sex. Even though I pressured him."

"Mother!"

"Oh, don't look so shocked! Everybody we knew was having sex, except the two of us. He thought we should wait."

"That says a lot about him," I say. "Any other guy..."

"Would have jumped at the chance," she says. "I know. Just another log on the fire. But not Tore. At the time, I thought it was because he didn't want to take advantage of me."

"And now...?"

"Now I see it was his way of saying he wasn't good enough for me. He knew I was meant for better things. And he didn't want to hold me back."

She's silent for a long time. We pass an exit. Then another exit. Finally, she speaks again.

"And then came graduation. It was always understood that I would be going off to college—very rare for a woman in Kongsvinger. But going to study in America? Almost unheard of."

"And Tore...?"

"He'd be staying home to take care of the family farm. But as the time grew closer, I didn't want to leave. Oh, I had some terrible fights with my family. But I didn't care. All I wanted was to be with Tore. And that's when he started pulling away."

"What did he do?"

"Suddenly made up all kinds of excuses why he couldn't see me. Tractor trouble. A fence needed painting. One of the cows was sick. I didn't understand. We had so little time left together. Why was he doing this? It was...the saddest I've ever been."

A man in a Kia is trying to pass me on the right.

Very annoying. I speed up, just to rile him. I wonder if I would be as angry at the guy right now...if he was a woman.

My mother looks at me for a long time. "Something else you should know," she says. "Something I never thought I'd tell you. I didn't think I could live without him. So one night, before I was scheduled to leave, I took a razor blade and—"

"Oh, no!" This is too sad. I don't want to hear any more. "But look how far you've come," I say. "All the things you've done, the awards, the people you've helped."

"Yes," she says, smiling. "I was so close to staying home. But Tore knew I wasn't cut out to be a farmer's wife, a small-town girl. He was sure I'd regret it, at some point, and he didn't want to be the cause of my unhappiness."

"And...Jeannie?"

"He spent a lot of time at our house when we were dating. And she adored him. She was always the shy klutzy kid sister, so he sort of took her under his wing—taught her to ride a bike, to roller skate."

"Sounds very big-brother-y."

"Yes it was...at first. But once I left, he still came by. She would write to me about it. It was all very above board at first. But then she began mentioning things they did together. Hayrides. A dance. A picnic down by the river."

"So you knew about them?"

She shrugs. "What can I say? She was there and I wasn't. No. Wait. That sounds way too opportunistic. The fact is, Jeannie was sweet and very pretty. Like him, she was a homebody. Still is. They were good for each other. Happy in their little lives, with no grandiose dreams. And I...went on to do what I was meant to do."

Yes, she did. And the world is a better place for it. But even now, almost fifty years later, I can hear a touch of sadness in her voice. My heart is breaking for her.

"And do you ever...I mean, are there times when...?" I don't know quite how to phrase this. So I bite the bullet and just come out with it. "Do you ever regret not marrying him?"

She smiles. "I can't quite see me spending my days milking cows, can you?" she asks.

"No," I say. "Not unless they make designer overalls." We both laugh at that.

But then she suddenly turns serious. "Besides, if I had stayed with him, I never would have had *you*."

Just in time, we arrive at our Oslo hotel. I wouldn't have been able to drive with the tears in my eyes. I circle around to the hotel entrance and wave to the bellhop, who pretends to remember us. Then I pop the trunk so he can get our luggage. My mother doesn't get out of the car. For a moment, she seems lost in thought.

"Love," she says as she unbuckles her seat belt.

"They say it's the last and most serious disease of childhood."

"Did you hear that from one of the pediatricians you work with?" I ask.

"Hardly." She smiles. "I think I once saw it on a coffee mug."

CHAPTER 58

SLOWLY, MY MOTHER SEEMS ready to put the past behind her and move on.

We spend our last day in Oslo shopping. We make a game of it: whatever she buys has to be shipped back to the States. I absolutely forbid her to get another suitcase.

Set my mother loose in a department store like Steen & Strøm and she's bound to find lots of things she can't live without. Today is no exception. She buys place mats, reindeer bookends, and a special Norwegian Christmas tree with tiny white lights. In another store: linen napkins in wonderful stripes of blue, violet, and green ("They'll remind me of the northern lights," she says), as well as a cheese slicer in the shape of a moose, and a few lucky trolls, all wearing tiny hand-knit sweaters. An Oleana knit coat and a matching dress. And in the local silver stores: a selection of belts, buckles, and pins.

Yes, she's being wildly acquisitive. But that beats a meltdown, anytime.

Time for lunch. We decide to share a *matpakke*, layers of fish and cheese served on dark wheat bread. We sit on a bench at the dock, watching the boats go by. Tourist season is over here. There's a definite chill in the air, and both of us are wearing our new sweaters. Other than the water lapping against the wooden pier, it's very quiet and peaceful. Time for reflecting.

"You know, compared to most people, you've had an amazing life," I tell her.

"Yes," she says. "I guess it turned out the way it was supposed to."

The Smartest Girl In The Class was destined to be out in the world, making a difference. I look at her profile against the sun. In spite of everything, I'm proud of her. Lots of good feelings come bubbling up: how determined she is; how strong. How people respect her, rely on her. And how, unlike most people, she hasn't let the vagaries of love drag her down. She doesn't wallow. She just dusts herself off and keeps going.

Whatever love my father gave her was all the love she needed; whatever love she gave me was all she had to give.

"By the way," I say, "Richard is back in Oslo. Do you mind if I meet him for dinner tonight?"

I expect a nod or an okay. I am totally shocked when she turns to me in anger.

"You stupid fool," she says.

What?

"Don't you realize he's just using you? You'll never see him again after today." Her voice is mean; her face radiates disgust. "I can't believe a daughter of mine could be so naïve."

I just sit there, with my mouth open. I thought she understood. I thought she got me. I thought...

"You're wrong!" I say. My voice is so loud, a few people on the dock look at me. But I don't care. "You're just jealous," I add.

"Of what?" she says. "Of *you*?"

Now the knives are coming out. "You felt betrayed," I say. "Yesterday you relived that pain all over again. And now you're taking it out on me!"

"That's ridiculous!"

"Is it? Just because you were tossed by the side of the road, doesn't mean I will be."

"I'm just looking out for you," she says.

"Really? Since when? Because I guess I didn't get the memo. All you care about...all you've *ever* cared about...is yourself."

Two weeks, hundreds of memories, thousands of dollars spent, and we're back to Square One. I'm amazed at how all those warm feelings that were bubbling up in me have turned into a tsunami of anger. I am furious.

"The whole world may adore you, but to me you're just a mean...selfish...miserable..." So many words come to mind. She's all of them. But I decide to leave it unfinished.

"Where are you going?" she asks as I get up. I don't answer.

I feel like I'm living in a *Peanuts* cartoon. Once again, Charlie Brown believes Lucy when she says she won't pull the football away. But of course, she does. So once again, Charlie Brown falls on his ass.

When will I ever learn?

CHAPTER 59

I REFUSE TO LET my mother's words ruin my evening with Richard. On the way back to the hotel, I practice the deep breathing Esther suggested for when I'm under stress. It works, sort of. I never had much patience for meditation. Besides, I'm way too agitated to meditate.

Back in the room, I take a warm lavender-scented bubble bath. It helps clear my mind. As I relax, I daydream of the night ahead. A nice uncomplicated evening with good food and great sex. Or maybe great food *and* great sex.

I'm tempted to double-lock the door, literally locking my mother out of my life. But I realize that's childish. Besides, she won't be back for a while. There are still a lot of stores she hasn't hit. I put the DO NOT DISTURB sign on the doorknob and start to get ready. Hair styled with a curling iron, lots of makeup carefully applied— moisturizers, primer, shadows, highlighters, bronzers, lip pumpers, the works. Then black slacks, a white silk blouse, and strappy black Louboutin heels.

I step back and check myself out in the mirror. I smile. Under other circumstances, my mother would be pleased to see how good I look.

For spite, I leave before she gets back so she won't get the chance.

Richard has texted me:

Thought you might want a change from Norwegian food. Indian ok? 5:00?

LMK. Xo. R.

He suggests Benares Indisk, an Indian restaurant a short walk from my hotel. I'm early, so I check my coat, sit down, and order a Flying Horse Royal Lager. I know nothing about it, but I like the name. The waitress brings it along with a basket of naan and some green sauce.

I look around. The chairs are upholstered in red velvet, the walls painted dark pink. Paintings of elephants and maharajas in turbans are everywhere, and there's a large Buddha sculpture on one side. The atmosphere is comfortable, and the food smells great. I'm at a nice corner table, so we'll still have a good deal of privacy.

Soon people begin to enter, mostly families with kids, and I realize I'm a tad overdressed. But I don't care. It's a little early for dinner, but that's fine. That means Richard and I will have more time together back at his hotel.

Then I see him at the door. I wave; he sees me and heads on over, then kisses me on the cheek.

"You look...smashing," he says.

"Why thank you, kind sir. And thanks for suggesting food from the other side of the world."

He smiles as he takes a seat. "I had a feeling you would be all fished and reindeered out by now."

"You are so right."

He dips a piece of naan into the green sauce. "Nothing like a little spicy curry to bring you back to reality. So, how was it? Do tell."

I fill him in on the northern lights and skim over the family reunion, purposely leaving out any mention of Tore.

"And were they glad to see you two?"

"Are you kidding? Dr. Liz is like a superstar there. It was like Odysseus returning to Penelope. Except my mother's odyssey was twice as long."

I expect him to ask if she behaved herself. He doesn't. He seems to have forgotten all about her meltdown. Oh, well. I'm surprised, but relieved. The less I think about her, the better.

"Shall we?" he asks, opening the menu. We skim it together, then decide to split an order of Kadhai Chicken with green chiles and pepper flakes, and something called Royal Lamb in Vegetable Sauce, plus a few popadams to start. A smiling waitress brings a martini for Richard and another Flying Horse for me.

We clink glasses with a simple "Cheers." Richard looks adorable, as usual, but a bit tired. Low-key. I'm sure he was up early this morning to catch his flight. It's probably jet lag.

"So," I say, hoping to amuse him. "I did a little reading about the anglerfish we ate last time."

"Indeed?"

"Yup. It turns out, once the male closes in on the female, he bites her belly and their tissues fuse together permanently."

"Ouch!" he says.

"Wait. It gets better. They're joined in what biologists call incredibly unholy matrimony. The guy is trapped. He stays there attached to his lady fish until he withers away and dies."

I was sure Richard would say something about this, either funny or sweet or sexually charged. But he doesn't. He's very quiet. I speak.

"Anyway, I'm glad you're here. I hope nothing terrible will happen in the office without you today."

"No," he says. "Nothing life-shattering."

The life-shattering part comes just as the waitress brings the popadams.

CHAPTER 60

"LISTEN," RICHARD SAYS. AND suddenly that sweet quirky smile I like so much disappears.

He takes a sip of his martini. Then another sip. Then a deep breath. Whatever he is about to say . . . I know I don't want to hear it.

"My God, you look lovely," he says. It's as if he's trying to convince himself into or out of something. "But you see, I haven't been totally honest with you."

He signals the waitress for a second martini.

"Remember 'the children'?" he asks. "From our first conversation?"

I think back to the night we met. *The children*. Right. The interns in his office.

"Actually, one of those interns—Cecily—is my daughter. She's twenty-one."

I wait, assuming there's more. There is.

"I have three daughters, actually. There's also Char-lotte, who's fourteen. And Eve, the baby—well, not really a baby, she'd kill me if she heard me describe her that way—just turned ten."

Daughters. So does that mean...?

At least he has the decency to look away. "And yes," he says. "I have a wife."

I'm waiting for him to add that they're divorced, or separated, or that she's suffering from an incurable disease. That they're having problems, or they have an arrangement. Even something as clichéd as she doesn't understand him.

He doesn't say any of that. Now I find myself sput-tering as much as he does. "Wh...why...why didn't you...?"

"Tell you, the first night we met? I couldn't. You were just so...irresistible. I was gobsmacked. Couldn't get you out of my mind."

I want to say something. But I'm having trouble breathing.

"I just *had* to be with you," he is saying. "And I would do it all again."

I would too, I think. Maybe that's why I am *this close* to tears.

"I should never have allowed it to get this far," he says. "But as the great Auden once wrote: the desires of the heart are as crooked as corkscrews."

"That's not fair!" I say, loud enough so that the

people at the next table turn and look at me. "You can't quote poetry when you're breaking up with someone! And you know what else is unfair?" I add. "All this time, you've been leading me on."

"No, Laurie. I was leading *myself* on. You're still young. You don't understand. It was thrilling to learn I could still feel that way about someone again. And the more time I spent with you...oh, bollocks. I wish we'd met years ago. Does that make sense?"

No. Nothing about this makes sense. The waitress must have stopped by at some point with our entrees. I don't know how long our lamb and our chicken have been sitting in front of us. I look around. The pink walls that seemed so pretty earlier are now nauseating. Why would anybody paint a restaurant the color of tongue? I'm getting faint just looking at them.

Our waitress reappears. She sees both our plates are untouched.

"Is everything all right?" she asks. Richard puts his hand across the table and tries to hold mine.

"No!" I say, pushing his hand away. The waitress thinks I'm talking to her.

"I'm sorry to hear that," she says. "What can I—"

"I mean, yes! Everything is fine. Lovely place, great service. Excuse me for a moment," I say as I get up from the table, pick up my purse, and go into the ladies' room. It's empty. I take a few deep breaths and throw some water on my face. A few more deep breaths, and the tears start falling. Is my mascara waterproof? Do I know? Do I give a damn?

I begin to talk to myself. "Okay, Laurie. This is bad. This is a disappointment. But you've gotten through worse. Your father's death was crushing. Losing Andrew was devastating. This is a guy you've seen just a couple of times. And if you attached more to it than that, it's your own fault."

I leave the ladies' room and head straight to the front door. Richard is on his phone and doesn't see me duck out. I grab my coat and walk as fast as my sexy-but-what-good-did-it-do-me Louboutin heels can carry me. Soon our hotel comes into view. I think about ducking into the lobby ladies' room to wipe off the eye makeup under my eyes, so my mother won't know I've been crying.

Oh, God. *My mother.* The last person on earth I want to see.

CHAPTER 61

TO MY MOTHER'S CREDIT, she is a total saint.

No *I-told-you-so*s. No *you're-better-off-without-hims*. Nothing but pure, honest sympathy from the moment I knock on her door and stand there crying.

I tell her about sitting across from Richard, joking about how male anglerfish hold on for dear life after sex... and how he suddenly remembered to tell me he's got three kids and a wife.

She listens without judging and without a single "Tsk, tsk." At one point she moves over and just holds me as I sit there and sob. How odd life is. A few hours ago, I was sure I'd never speak to her again. Suddenly she's morphed into the mother I always wanted.

"I don't know what to do," I blubber between sobs.

"I do," she says.

She goes to the hotel phone. It's almost six thirty, and the hotel spa closes at seven. But with her usual charm and persistence, my mother manages to get them to keep it open a little longer, just for the two of us. I don't even want to ask what this will cost.

"Our aim here is to get your body to release more serotonin," she says in her best Dr. Liz voice. "Serotonin is known as the happiness hormone. And the evidence is not just anecdotal."

Sure. Fine. Whatever.

Within minutes, we're stripping down in the hotel spa dressing room and heading to the *badstue,* a cedar-scented sauna where the temperature is over a hundred and fifty degrees. Every few minutes an attendant opens the door and spills a pitcher of water on a pail of hot rocks, creating a cloud of hissing steam. It's hard to breathe at first.

"Lie down on the bench," my mother says. "Let the steam surround your whole body." So I do. I begin to sweat a little, then a lot. A bell goes off a few minutes later. Our sauna is over.

"Feeling any better?" my mother asks.

"Nowhere near happy," I say. "But maybe a tad less miserable."

"Don't worry," she says. "That was just the beginning."

Next, still naked, we're side by side on adjacent gurneys. Modest paper doilies cover our private parts, and tiny blackout sunglasses cover our eyes. Liv and

Elsa, our two personal attendants, proceed to give us a head-to-toe anti-stress exfoliating salt scrub to stimulate circulation. Then they hose us down as if our bodies were on fire.

Next comes a full-body "facial." We have a choice of either mud or seaweed.

As the queen of self-indulgence, my mother knows all about pampering. I let her decide.

"Seaweed," she says. So Liv and Elsa smear on a gluey green mixture of seaweed, kelp, amino acids, and vitamins, then leave us alone for a while to marinate.

"Why did you pick seaweed?" I ask.

"It's an anti-inflammatory," she says. "And it rids your body of toxins." *Good call. Richard was pretty toxic, now that I think about it.* I like the idea of my body squeezing him out of every pore.

Once the seaweed hardens, they wipe it off with wet cloths and slather on a delicious almond-scented moisturizer. Then it's time for a hydrating beverage: a seaweed-based juice drink. It smells fishy and tastes like the ocean. I try not to grimace after I take a sip. It's disgusting. Dr. Liz, of course, chugs hers down.

But wait, as all those late-night infomercials say. *There's more!*

A manicure. A pedicure. And a *total head-conditioning treatment.* Not just hair. *Total. Head.* Elsa sounds like she speaks in italics as she describes these treatments.

My very first *scalp assessment* has revealed that I have a *scaly scalp* that can *slow hair growth,* which is why I suffer from *unruly hair.* Who knew? She recommends a *special Omega-3 fatty acid treatment* to calm my scalp and stimulate hair follicles.

Maybe I should hire her to help me write Boujee shampoo commercials.

It's almost midnight. I'm exhausted. By the time I get back to the room, my endorphins are racing around inside me like little hormonal Hot Wheels. I must admit, I'm feeling better.

Tomorrow we fly back to America. So tonight, since I'm almost on the verge of cheerful, I decide to make a list of all the good things about being dumped—by a cheating jerk like Richard.

REASONS I AM REALLY GLAD IT DIDN'T WORK OUT

He's a liar. Not even a recovering liar. A *real* liar.

His adorableness is going to look kind of cheesy when he's sixty.

I didn't want to move to London. I like my New York apartment, my New York job, my New York life. (NOTE TO SELF: Start texting some friends about him, so they can help you hate him.)

All those cute British slang words he uses—*bollocks, gobsmacked*—would start to get on my nerves.

I'd have to invite all his boring lawyer "mates" for dinner.

We'd argue about his ex-wife and kids.
How could I ever trust him? (See Number 1.)
I was never *really* in love with him. Just a little in love.
He dresses better than I do.
He probably eats blood sausages.

CHAPTER 62

THE CONCIERGE HIRES AN SUV to get us to the airport. Even though the vehicle is huge, there's barely enough room for all my mother's luggage.

I bought a total of *one* bulky hand-knit sweater while in Norway. She has bought seven. Rather than pack them all, she decides we will each wear four. So we do. We look at each other and laugh. We look like dropouts from *The Biggest Loser*.

Oslo's Gardermoen Airport is fairly empty. We waddle through security. Once on board our SAS flight, we take off our sweaters and use them as seat cushions.

What a trip this has been!

I look at my mother. Her hair is bouncy. Her skin is glowing. *(Shout-out here to Liv, to Elsa, and to seaweed.)* Even better, she's all smiles. She seems really happy.

I'm happy, too. Happy to put the whole Richard mess behind me. But also happy that Richard showed me there's Life After Andrew. Somewhere in the future, I know there'll be a Life After Richard.

"This has been wonderful," my mother says. "Who would have guessed..."

"That we'd get along so well?" I ask.

"Not just get along. Really *enjoy* each other."

"With only two meltdowns the whole time."

"Two meltdowns in fourteen days? Not bad for us," she says.

"Yes," I say. "I think that must be some sort of record."

The captain announces that we are number one for takeoff, and soon the plane begins to move forward. For the second time in two weeks, my mother recites her grandmother's Norwegian travel poem. Then she leans over and takes my hand, even though there's no turbulence.

What a fabulous trip this has been.

CHAPTER 63

YES, IT WAS A fabulous trip.

How I wish it had actually happened that way.

But you know the old saying: *If you want to make God laugh, tell Him your plans.*

Here's what really happened after I was summoned to my mother's hospital bedside in New Jersey:

My mother agreed to stay in the hospital one more day for further tests. The next day, Dr. Malcolm Akers was already there when I arrived. He was going over the results with her. He looked concerned.

"The MRI shows you definitely had a silent heart attack," he was telling my mother. "That happens when—"

"I *know* how it happens," she interrupted him, curtly. So he turned to me.

"It's when blood flow to the heart is temporarily blocked," Dr. Akers said as I sat there taking notes. "It's a heart attack with no symptoms, minimal symptoms, or unrecognized symptoms. There's no pain—"

"You're forgetting that I came in here *with pain* on Sunday night," she said, interrupting again.

"Elizabeth!" Dr. Akers snapped. It was clear he was losing patience with her. Akers had the tone of voice you use for a dog who has misbehaved. "The *degree* of cardiac scarring and damage I'm seeing *did not happen* on Sunday."

That quieted my mother for a moment or two. He continued speaking to her as if she were a normal patient. *As if.*

"Any bouts of indigestion? Shortness of breath? Jaw pain?"

"No, no, and no," she said, clearly annoyed at the questions.

He's looked at her chart. "I see you play tennis...don't smoke...you're not overweight...blood pressure within normal range. All good. Any extra stress lately?"

"Only for the last thirty years."

He ignored her sarcasm. "Any family history of heart disease?"

The moment of truth. "My mother," she said, frowning. Then added, "And my father."

Dr. Akers's frown was now bigger than hers. "I want you to start on 325 mg aspirin every night. I'm writing you a prescription for 90 mg of Brilinta, once a day."

"Not Plavix?"

"Not when a patient is on Prozac."

Wait. What? My tough, hard-boiled mother is on Prozac? *Since when? Why?*

But there was no time to ask. I scribbled away, trying to get down all the info Dr. Akers was rattling off about *platelets, ischemia, triglycerides, low-density lipoproteins, a possible carotid stent, diet restrictions…*

On the word *diet*, my mother smirked. "Impossible," she said. "My daughter and I are heading to Paris."

"And you want me to give you a hall pass?"

"You don't have to. I'll give myself one."

Then it was his turn to smirk. "You're a big girl, Elizabeth. I can't make you do anything you don't care to do. But I would advise you to stay put here until the rest of your test results come in."

He left.

"I'll come by again tomorrow," I said to my mother, kissing her still-somewhat-angry face. "And if they say you can go…"

"We…are…going!" she said.

It was the last thing she ever said to me.

CHAPTER 64

THREE IN THE MORNING. I'm asleep. The phone rings. Never a good sign.

"Is this Laurie Margolis?" a voice asks.

"Yes..."

"This is Miriam Kirsten from Ridgefield Hospital. I'm calling because your mother..."

Four minutes. That's all the time it takes me to dress, run out of my apartment, and jump into a cab. There is no traffic on the drive from Manhattan to the hospital. Still, the trip feels like hours.

When I get to my mother's room, she's unconscious. Her eyes are closed; her breathing is ragged, even with an oxygen mask. She is hooked up to machines that are flashing, beeping, pumping. Several doctors and nurses crowd around her, silent.

This can't be happening, I think. *Not to me. Not to my mother.*

Yet that's my mother lying there, her mouth open, scarcely breathing. And that's me, standing by her side, also scarcely breathing. They want me to leave the room, but I can't. I won't. Instead, I push myself between two people to get closer to her.

"She's on morphine," someone tells me. "She won't know you're here." I don't believe that. I take her hand. I squeeze it. I wait a moment. She squeezes back. I breathe a sigh of relief. *See? She knows I'm here! She's going to be okay! She's determined to get her strength back so that she and I... the two of us can...*

Suddenly everything stops. The room gets very quiet.

"I'm sorry," one of the doctors says.

What?

"I'm sorry," he says again.

I don't understand. What does he mean?

"That pain she presented with on Sunday was cardiac arrest. We were able to *something, something, something*. But then she *something* and *something else* and we couldn't..."

I'm feeling faint. Quickly, they lead me to a chair. Someone cracks open a vial and holds it under my nose. It hurts. It burns. My eyes tear. I don't faint, but I'm still dizzy. They want me to bend my head down between my knees and take some deep breaths. I do at first. But then I get up. I want to hold my mother's hand again. It's a little cooler than before. But I'm sure if I keep squeezing, and if I wait...

Time passes. People come in and out. Several people—doctors? nurses?—try to comfort me, saying nice things, kind things. I don't remember any of them.

Someone hands me a big plastic shopping bag so I can pack up all my mother's belongings. Her La Perla bra . . . her bespoke Burberry raincoat . . . a Carolina Herrera cashmere sweater and pencil skirt. I fold every piece slowly and carefully. I know she'll be angry if anything gets wrinkled.

I find her cell phone in her nightstand drawer along with everything the hospital has provided: a small bottle of mouthwash, a plastic bowl, a toothbrush, a tiny tube of toothpaste suited for a dollhouse, and a minuscule bottle of hand lotion.

But as I'm tossing all that except the phone in the garbage, I see something underneath. A sealed envelope on which are written two words: *For Laurie.*

CHAPTER 65

THE HOSPITAL HAS GIVEN me pages and pages of forms to read and sign. I'll do that later when I get home, or tomorrow when I get up.

But for now, I need to read what my mother wrote. Even seeing her handwriting on the envelope makes me choke up. But I can't put it off any longer.

I open it.

Dear Laurie,

I want you to know how touched I was by your wonderful gesture.

My daughter wants to travel with me! Is there anything better a mother can hear? I don't think so. I'm sitting here in a room the color of clotted pea soup, wearing one of those hideous hospital gowns...but I can't stop smiling.

How you lifted my spirits! I know you think I'm invincible. I always thought so myself. But as of Sunday night I'm not so sure. Even now, sitting here smiling my face off as I think about our trip, I'm feeling—I don't know. A little off? Something is not quite right.

Maybe it's that I've been in thousands of hospital rooms over the years, but never horizontal. It definitely changes one's perspective of...well, everything. I can't wait to get out of here and go soaring off to Europe with you, the moment Dr. Akers says I can.

But if for some reason I can't...

Laurie: you must go on our trip by yourself. And you must write our story—the story of the trip we would have had.

Make it honest. Make it funny. Above all else, make it real. You can do it. You're a wonderful writer. And you know better than anybody the things we'd laugh about. Argue about. Meals we'd have. Things we'd learn. I'm sure we'd have had a couple of fights, and that's fine too. We're bound to disagree about pretty much everything. That's us: the mother-daughter Odd Couple.

I know what you're thinking: why is she asking this? I can't possibly do that. But the truth is, you can and you must. Paris is good for the soul. It will help you heal.

And you must, must visit the land I grew up in, my hometown, the family you barely know you have. Meeting them will teach you so much you never knew about me. They'll love you. They loved me, too. That's another reason to go: you won't have to mourn alone.

A confession here—though I doubt I'm telling you anything you don't already know: I was a much better doctor than mother. I hope, as time passes, you'll forgive me for the things I did and the things I didn't do. If I had it to do over...

Except I don't. None of us ever does.

With any luck, we'll soon be on our merry way and you will never have to read this. But if you do...

Something I never told you nearly enough: how much I love you.

xo

CHAPTER 66

OH, MOTHER. IT HAS been almost four years since you wrote that. And you've missed out on so much.

I railed against your suggestion at first. I thought it was crazy. I was too sad, too scared to go alone. And I was angry at you for dying, for cheating me out of a chance to really get to know you.

My therapist and I discussed it a lot. You never met Esther, but she's a wise and thoughtful woman who has been a great comfort to me. She agreed I should go on the trip without you. She thought writing about it would help me grieve. And she really liked the idea of me meeting your family.

"Your mother was right," she said. "It will do you good to surround yourself with people who've missed her all these years—maybe as much as you do."

As the child of a mixed marriage, I mourned you in two separate ways. First, a service at Bethel Lutheran

Church—packed, you'll be glad to know. Pastor Knutson gave a beautiful sermon about grace, forgiveness, and doing God's work here on earth. I read aloud an Emily Dickinson poem that seemed so perfect for the way you lived your life:

Because I could not stop for death—
He kindly stopped for me—

After the burial, I mourned you a second way, the Jewish way. I went back to your apartment and sat Shiva for five days.

When I was going through your papers, I found the travel prayer your grandmother gave you all those years ago. I brought it with me on the plane to Paris. And when we hit some turbulence, I pretended you were reading it to me.

I tried to make our story as authentic as I could. That meant putting in a lot of shopping, several arguments, two major meltdowns, an unconscionable amount of great meals, and a lot of touching moments. So many times, I found myself asking, *What would my mother have to say about this?*, and I had to smile, knowing *exactly* what you would say.

And I did meet a man in Paris—a whirlwind romance I was sure would travel across the pond. Alas, it did not. I wrote about that, too. I think you would be pleased with how "motherly" I thought you'd be, when I showed up at your door, heartbroken. How close the two of us became, toward the end.

Visiting your family was wonderful. The minute I met your sister Jeannie, I felt like I'd known her forever. I wound up staying for a week, during which time we went through countless photo albums and countless bottles of aquavit. They told me all about your life there, and what happened at the end. They've missed you all these years. But they always understood your reluctance to return.

Tore had tears in his eyes when he hugged me hello. He thinks I look like you. He's an old man now, but even when he was sharing funny memories, there was a touch of wistfulness in his voice.

I think I can safely say: he has never forgotten you.

Enough endings. Let me tell you about new beginnings.

A year after your death, I met Rob, my friend Lynda's brother. She swore that the two of us would hit it off, but I was reluctant. He's twelve years older than I am, for one thing, and never married. Two red flags, in my book. But she wore me down. I said yes.

Rob Murray, it turns out, was—is—a gem. Kind, warm, and absolutely devoted to me. You would love him. Dad would too. (Remember how he used to judge all my boyfriends by the firmness of their handshake? Rob has a great one.)

When we got married, I was thirty-eight. Rob was fifty. When people ask why he never married before, he smiles and says, "I was waiting for Laurie."

We have a little boy now. He's almost two—spunky, friendly, tough as nails, and determined to have his own way. Sound familiar? And of course, I named him after you: Eli Ormson Murray.

Dear Mother: there is so much I never got to tell you, share with you, say to you.

So instead, I have plenty of conversations with you in my head. When in doubt, I always ask myself, "What would Dr. Liz do?" Sometimes I follow your advice, and sometimes I don't.

It's only now, years later, that I've begun to realize all you taught me, and what a role model you were. Maybe the most important thing I learned from you: people don't always give you what you want. They give you what they have to give.

But if you stop and think about it, that can be enough.

AUTHORS' NOTE

On paper, our two mothers could not be more different.

Lorraine Minerva Ormson (Sue's mom) grew up on a farm in New Lisbon, Wisconsin. My mom, Geraldine Gelbaum, grew up in an apartment in the Bronx.

Sue's mom graduated from the University of Wisconsin-Madison, a rare achievement for a woman in 1943. Even rarer: she double majored in economics and nursing, became a Professor of Nursing, and then became head nurse at Wisconsin General Hospital, University of Wisconsin-Madison.

My mother studied bookkeeping in high school. She modeled for a while after graduation, then went to work in a New York law firm.

Lorraine turned down several marriage proposals until she met a fellow Badger, Orville Berthold Solie ("OB"). She and OB were married for fifty-four years, until he died. She died the day before what would have been their sixty-sixth wedding anniversary.

My mother lost her first husband (my dad, Joseph Katz, an attorney) when she was forty-three. She lost her second (Alfred DeResta, a jewelry designer) when she was sixty. She spent the rest of her life looking for a third.

Lorraine, a serious runner and bridge player, loved college football and golf, math and March Madness—maybe because she was born in March. Geraldine, a serious knitter and mah jong whiz, also born in March, was a fan of old movies, new clothes, and January White Sales.

Both were devoted to their grandchildren, of course, impressing upon all of them the importance of gratitude and thank-you notes, kindness, and optimism.

But the major wonderful thing they had in common: both had daughters who adored them and who were crushed when they died—ironically, within a year of one another.

Lorraine started going downhill after a fall. Geraldine was never the same after a stroke. Both were in their nineties. Their deaths should not have come as such a shock.

But of course, it always does.

How delighted they'd be, if they were still around, to hear what their grandchildren have been up to. The trendy jobs they hold, the loves they've found, the baby one of them is expecting.

We would tell them how much their wisdom and support still resonates with the two of us, helping us craft the lives we have now as writers, artists, and mothers.

Most of all: we could show them the book we created in their honor. The story of a mother and daughter who learn how to love and talk to each other before it's too late.

And how that book is lovingly dedicated to the two of them, Lorraine and Geraldine.

ABOUT THE AUTHORS

Susan Solie Patterson has a Bachelor of Science/Master of Fine Arts degree from the University of Wisconsin-Madison, where she was also an All-American swimmer. She is the author of *Big Words for Little Geniuses*, a *New York Times* bestseller.

Susan DiLallo is a lyricist, librettist, humor columnist, and former advertising creative director. She is the author of *The House Next Door*, a *New York Times* bestseller. She lives in New York City with her family.

James Patterson is the world's bestselling author. The creator of Alex Cross, he has produced more enduring fictional heroes than any other novelist alive. He lives in Florida with his family.

Also By James Patterson

ALEX CROSS NOVELS

Along Came a Spider • Kiss the Girls • Jack and Jill • Cat and
Mouse • Pop Goes the Weasel • Roses are Red • Violets are
Blue • Four Blind Mice • The Big Bad Wolf • London Bridges •
Mary, Mary • Cross • Double Cross • Cross Country • Alex
Cross's Trial (*with Richard DiLallo*) • I, Alex Cross • Cross Fire •
Kill Alex Cross • Merry Christmas, Alex Cross • Alex Cross,
Run • Cross My Heart • Hope to Die • Cross Justice • Cross
the Line • The People vs. Alex Cross • Target: Alex Cross •
Criss Cross • Deadly Cross • Fear No Evil • Triple Cross

THE WOMEN'S MURDER CLUB SERIES

1st to Die (*with Andrew Gross*) • 2nd Chance (*with Andrew
Gross*) • 3rd Degree (*with Andrew Gross*) • 4th of July (*with
Maxine Paetro*) • The 5th Horseman (*with Maxine Paetro*) • The
6th Target (*with Maxine Paetro*) • 7th Heaven (*with Maxine
Paetro*) • 8th Confession (*with Maxine Paetro*) • 9th Judgement
(*with Maxine Paetro*) • 10th Anniversary (*with Maxine Paetro*) •
11th Hour (*with Maxine Paetro*) • 12th of Never (*with Maxine
Paetro*) • Unlucky 13 (*with Maxine Paetro*) • 14th Deadly Sin
(*with Maxine Paetro*) • 15th Affair (*with Maxine Paetro*) • 16th
Seduction (*with Maxine Paetro*) • 17th Suspect (*with Maxine
Paetro*) • 18th Abduction (*with Maxine Paetro*) • 19th
Christmas (*with Maxine Paetro*) • 20th Victim (*with Maxine
Paetro*) • 21st Birthday (*with Maxine Paetro*) • 22 Seconds
(*with Maxine Paetro*) • 23rd Midnight (*with Maxine Paetro*)

DETECTIVE MICHAEL BENNETT SERIES

Step on a Crack (*with Michael Ledwidge*) • Run for Your Life
(*with Michael Ledwidge*) • Worst Case (*with Michael Ledwidge*) •
Tick Tock (*with Michael Ledwidge*) • I, Michael Bennett (*with
Michael Ledwidge*) • Gone (*with Michael Ledwidge*) • Burn (*with
Michael Ledwidge*) • Alert (*with Michael Ledwidge*) • Bullseye
(*with Michael Ledwidge*) • Haunted (*with James O. Born*) •
Ambush (*with James O. Born*) • Blindside (*with James O. Born*) •
The Russian (*with James O. Born*) • Shattered (*with James O. Born*)

PRIVATE NOVELS

Private (*with Maxine Paetro*) • Private London (*with Mark Pearson*) • Private Games (*with Mark Sullivan*) • Private: No. 1 Suspect (*with Maxine Paetro*) • Private Berlin (*with Mark Sullivan*) • Private Down Under (*with Michael White*) • Private L.A. (*with Mark Sullivan*) • Private India (*with Ashwin Sanghi*) • Private Vegas (*with Maxine Paetro*) • Private Sydney (*with Kathryn Fox*) • Private Paris (*with Mark Sullivan*) • The Games (*with Mark Sullivan*) • Private Delhi (*with Ashwin Sanghi*) • Private Princess (*with Rees Jones*) • Private Moscow (*with Adam Hamdy*) • Private Rogue (*with Adam Hamdy*) • Private Beijing (*with Adam Hamdy*)

NYPD RED SERIES

NYPD Red (*with Marshall Karp*) • NYPD Red 2 (*with Marshall Karp*) • NYPD Red 3 (*with Marshall Karp*) • NYPD Red 4 (*with Marshall Karp*) • NYPD Red 5 (*with Marshall Karp*) • NYPD Red 6 (*with Marshall Karp*)

DETECTIVE HARRIET BLUE SERIES

Never Never (*with Candice Fox*) • Fifty Fifty (*with Candice Fox*) • Liar Liar (*with Candice Fox*) • Hush Hush (*with Candice Fox*)

INSTINCT SERIES

Instinct (*with Howard Roughan, previously published as Murder Games*) • Killer Instinct (*with Howard Roughan*) • Steal (*with Howard Roughan*)

THE BLACK BOOK SERIES

The Black Book (*with David Ellis*) • The Red Book (*with David Ellis*) • Escape (*with David Ellis*)

STAND-ALONE THRILLERS

The Thomas Berryman Number • Hide and Seek • Black Market • The Midnight Club • Sail (*with Howard Roughan*) • Swimsuit (*with Maxine Paetro*) • Don't Blink (*with Howard

Roughan) • Postcard Killers (*with Liza Marklund*) • Toys (*with Neil McMahon*) • Now You See Her (*with Michael Ledwidge*) • Kill Me If You Can (*with Marshall Karp*) • Guilty Wives (*with David Ellis*) • Zoo (*with Michael Ledwidge*) • Second Honeymoon (*with Howard Roughan*) • Mistress (*with David Ellis*) • Invisible (*with David Ellis*) • Truth or Die (*with Howard Roughan*) • Murder House (*with David Ellis*) • The Store (*with Richard DiLallo*) • Texas Ranger (*with Andrew Bourelle*) • The President is Missing (*with Bill Clinton*) • Revenge (*with Andrew Holmes*) • Juror No. 3 (*with Nancy Allen*) • The First Lady (*with Brendan DuBois*) • The Chef (*with Max DiLallo*) • Out of Sight (*with Brendan DuBois*) • Unsolved (*with David Ellis*) • The Inn (*with Candice Fox*) • Lost (*with James O. Born*) • Texas Outlaw (*with Andrew Bourelle*) • The Summer House (*with Brendan DuBois*) • 1st Case (*with Chris Tebbetts*) • Cajun Justice (*with Tucker Axum*)• The Midwife Murders (*with Richard DiLallo*) • The Coast-to-Coast Murders (*with J.D. Barker*) • Three Women Disappear (*with Shan Serafin*) • The President's Daughter (*with Bill Clinton*) • The Shadow (*with Brian Sitts*) • The Noise (*with J.D. Barker*) • 2 Sisters Detective Agency (*with Candice Fox*) • Jailhouse Lawyer (*with Nancy Allen*) • The Horsewoman (*with Mike Lupica*) • Run Rose Run (*with Dolly Parton*) • Death of the Black Widow (*with J.D. Barker*) • The Ninth Month (*with Richard DiLallo*) • The Girl in the Castle (*with Emily Raymond*) • Blowback (*with Brendan DuBois*) • The Twelve Topsy-Turvy, Very Messy Days of Christmas (*with Tad Safran*) • The Perfect Assassin (*with Brian Sitts*) • House of Wolves (*with Mike Lupica*) • Countdown (*with Brendan DuBois*)

NON-FICTION

Torn Apart (*with Hal and Cory Friedman*) • The Murder of King Tut (*with Martin Dugard*) • All-American Murder (*with Alex Abramovich and Mike Harvkey*) • The Kennedy Curse (*with Cynthia Fagen*) • The Last Days of John Lennon (*with Casey Sherman and Dave Wedge*) • Walk in My Combat Boots (*with Matt Eversmann and Chris Mooney*) • ER Nurses (*with Matt Eversmann*) • James Patterson by James Patterson: The Stories of My Life • Diana, William and Harry (*with Chris Mooney*) • American Cops (*with Matt Eversmann*)

MURDER IS FOREVER TRUE CRIME

Murder, Interrupted (*with Alex Abramovich and Christopher Charles*) • Home Sweet Murder (*with Andrew Bourelle and Scott Slaven*) • Murder Beyond the Grave (*with Andrew Bourelle and Christopher Charles*) • Murder Thy Neighbour (*with Andrew Bourelle and Max DiLallo*) • Murder of Innocence (*with Max DiLallo and Andrew Bourelle*) • Till Murder Do Us Part (*with Andrew Bourelle and Max DiLallo*)

COLLECTIONS

Triple Threat (*with Max DiLallo and Andrew Bourelle*) • Kill or Be Killed (*with Maxine Paetro, Rees Jones, Shan Serafin and Emily Raymond*) • The Moores are Missing (*with Loren D. Estleman, Sam Hawken and Ed Chatterton*) • The Family Lawyer (*with Robert Rotstein, Christopher Charles and Rachel Howzell Hall*) • Murder in Paradise (*with Doug Allyn, Connor Hyde and Duane Swierczynski*) • The House Next Door (*with Susan DiLallo, Max DiLallo and Brendan DuBois*) • 13-Minute Murder (*with Shan Serafin, Christopher Farnsworth and Scott Slaven*) • The River Murders (*with James O. Born*) • The Palm Beach Murders (*with James O. Born, Duane Swierczynski and Tim Arnold*) • Paris Detective • 3 Days to Live

For more information about James Patterson's novels, visit www.penguin.co.uk.